## BEFORE SHE MET ME

Julian Barnes is the author of eleven novels, including *Metroland*, *Flaubert's Parrot*, *A History of the World in 10½ Chapters* and *Arthur & George*. His most recent novel, *The Sense of an Ending*, won the 2011 Man Booker Prize for Fiction. He has also written three books of short stories, *Cross Channel*, *The Lemon Table* and *Pulse*; and three collections of journalism, *Letters from London*, *Something to Declare* and *The Pedant in the Kitchen*. His latest book, *Levels of Life*, was published in 2013 and was a *Sunday Times* Number One bestseller. His work has been translated into more than thirty languages. In France he is the only writer to have won both the Prix Médicis (for *Flaubert's Parrot*) and the Prix Femina (for *Talking it Over*). In 2004 he received the Austrian State Prize for European Literature, and in 2011 he was awarded the David Cohen Prize for Literature. He lives in London.

Also by Julian Barnes

Fiction

*Metroland*

*Flaubert's Parrot*

*Staring at the Sun*

*A History of the World in 10½ Chapters*

*Talking it Over*

*The Porcupine*

*Cross Channel*

*England, England*

*Love, etc*

*The Lemon Table*

*Arthur & George*

*Pulse*

*The Sense of an Ending*

Non-fiction

*Letters from London 1990–1995*

*Something to Declare*

*The Pedant in the Kitchen*

*Nothing to be Frightened of*

*Levels of Life*

Translation

*In the Land of Pain*

*by Alphonse Daudet*

# JULIAN BARNES

# Before She Met Me

**VINTAGE BOOKS**
London

Published by Vintage 2009

6 8 10 9 7 5

First published in Great Britain in 1982 by Jonathan Cape

Vintage
Random House, 20 Vauxhall Bridge Road,
London, SW1V 2SA

www.vintage-books.co.uk

Addresses for companies within The Random House Group Limited
can be found at: www.randomhouse.co.uk/offices.htm

The Random House Group Limited Reg. No. 954009

A CIP catalogue record for this book
is available from the British Library

ISBN 9780099540076

The Random House Group Limited supports The Forest Stewardship
Council® (FSC®), the leading international forest-certification organisation.
Our books carrying the FSC label are printed on FSC®-certified paper.
FSC is the only forest-certification scheme supported by the leading
environmental organisations, including Greenpeace. Our
paper procurement policy can be found at
www.randomhouse.co.uk/environment

MIX
Paper from
responsible sources
FSC
www.fsc.org    FSC® C016897

Printed and bound in Great Britain by Clays Ltd, St Ives plc

*To Pat*

Man finds himself in the predicament that nature has endowed him essentially with three brains which, despite great differences in structure, must function together and communicate with one another. The oldest of these brains is basically reptilian. The second has been inherited from the lower mammals, and the third is a late mammalian development, which ... has made man peculiarly man. Speaking allegorically of these brains within a brain, we might imagine that when the psychiatrist bids the patient to lie on the couch, he is asking him to stretch out alongside a horse and a crocodile.

Paul D. MacLean, *Journal of Nervous and Mental Diseases*, Vol. CXXXV, No 4, October 1962

*Il vaut mieux encore être marié qu'être mort.*

Molière, *Les Fourberies de Scapin.*

# Contents

ONE    Three Suits and a Violin    11

TWO    *In flagrante*    29

THREE    The Cross-Eyed Bear    42

FOUR    Sansepolcro, Poggibonsi    56

FIVE    Sawn-Offs and Four-Eyes    69

SIX    Mister Carwash    85

SEVEN    On the Dunghill    104

EIGHT    The Feminian Sandstones    118

NINE    Sometimes a Cigar …    140

TEN    The Stanley Spencer Syndrome    154

ELEVEN    The Horse and the Crocodile    169

# ONE

# Three Suits and a Violin

The first time Graham Hendrick watched his wife commit adultery he didn't mind at all. He even found himself chuckling. It never occurred to him to reach out a shielding hand towards his daughter's eyes.

Of course, Barbara was behind it. Barbara, his first wife; as opposed to Ann, his second wife — the one who was committing the adultery. Though naturally, at the time he didn't think of it as adultery. So the response of *pas devant* wasn't appropriate. And in any case, it was still what Graham called the honey time.

The honey time had begun on April 22nd, 1977, at Repton Gardens, when Jack Lupton introduced him to a girl parachutist. He was on his third drink of the party. But alcohol never helped him relax: as soon as Jack introduced the girl, something flickered in his brain and automatically expunged her name. That was what happened at parties. A few years earlier, as an experiment, Graham had tried repeating the person's name as they shook hands. 'Hullo, Rachel,' he'd say, and 'Hullo, Lionel,' and 'Good evening, Marion.' But the men seemed to think you homosexual for it, and eyed you warily; while the women asked politely if you were Bostonian, or, perhaps, a Positive Thinker. Graham had abandoned the technique and gone back to feeling ashamed of his brain.

On that warm April night, leaning against Jack's bookshelves and away from the turmoil of warbling smokers,

Graham gazed civilly across at this still anonymous woman with neatly-shaped blondeish hair and a candy-striped shirt that was silk for all he knew.

'It must be an interesting life.'

'Yes, it is.'

'You must ... travel around a lot.'

'Yes, I do.'

'Give demonstrations, I suppose.' He imagined her cartwheeling through the air while scarlet smoke hissed from a canister strapped to her ankle.

'Well, that's the other department, really.' (What department was that?)

'It must be dangerous, though.'

'What — you mean ... the flying?' Surprising, Ann thought, how often men were scared of aeroplanes. They never bothered her.

'No, not the flying bit, the other bit. The jumping.'

Ann put her head on one side by way of interrogation.

'The jumping.' Graham placed his glass on a shelf and flapped his arms up and down. Ann put her head further on one side. He grasped the middle button of his jacket and gave it a sharp, military downward tug.

'Ah,' he said finally, 'thought you were a parachutist.' The lower half of Ann's face formed itself into a smile, then her eyes moved slowly from sceptical pity to amusement. '*Jack* said you were a parachutist,' he repeated, as if the reiteration and the attributed authority made it more likely to be true. In fact, of course, the opposite was the case. It was doubtless another example of what Jack called 'making the knees-up go with a swing you silly old cunt'.

'So in that case,' she replied, 'you aren't a historian and you don't teach at London University.'

'Good God no,' said Graham. 'Do I look like an academic?'

'I don't know what they look like. Don't they look like everybody else?'

'No they don't,' said Graham, quite fiercely. 'They wear glasses and brown tweed jackets and have humps on their backs and mean, jealous natures and they all use Old Spice.' Ann looked at him. He had glasses and a brown corduroy jacket.

'I'm a brain surgeon,' he said. 'Well, not really. I'm working my way up. You have to practise on other bits first: stands to reason. I'm on shoulders and necks at the moment.'

'That must be interesting,' she said, uncertain how far to disbelieve him. 'It must be difficult,' she added.

'It is difficult.' He shifted his glasses on his nose, moving them sideways before settling them back exactly where they had been before. He was tall, with an elongated, squared-off face and dark brown hair erratically touched with grey, as if someone had shaken it from a clogging pepper pot. 'It's also dangerous.'

'I should think it is.' No wonder his hair was like that.

'The most dangerous part,' he explained, 'is the flying.'

She smiled; he smiled. She wasn't just pretty; she was friendly as well.

'I'm a buyer,' she said, 'I buy clothes.'

'I'm an academic,' he said. 'I teach history at London University.'

'I'm a magician,' said Jack Lupton, loafing at the edge of their conversation and now canting a bottle into the middle of it. 'I teach magic at the University of Life. Wine or wine?'

'Go away, Jack,' said Graham, firmly for him. And Jack had gone away.

Looking back, Graham could see with urgent clarity how beached his life had been at that time. Unless, of course, urgent clarity was always a deceptive function of looking back. He had been thirty-eight then: fifteen years married; ten years in the same job; halfway through an elastic mortgage. Halfway through life as well, he supposed; and he could feel the downhill slope already.

Not that Barbara would have seen it like this. And not

that he could have expressed it to her like this either. Perhaps that was part of the trouble.

He was still fond of Barbara at the time; though he hadn't really loved her, hadn't felt anything like pride, or even interest, in their relationship, for at least five years. He was fond of their daughter Alice; though, somewhat to his surprise, she had never excited any very deep emotions in him. He was glad when she did well at school, but doubted if this gladness was really distinguishable from relief that she wasn't doing badly: how could you tell? He was negatively fond of his job too; though a bit less fond each year, as the students he processed became callower, more guiltlessly lazy and more politely unreachable than ever.

Throughout the fifteen years of his marriage, he'd never been unfaithful to Barbara: because he thought it was wrong, but also, he supposed, because he'd never really been tempted (when gusset-flashing girl students crossed their legs at him, he responded by giving them the more difficult essay options; they passed on the news that he was a cold fish). In the same way, he'd never thought of shifting his job, and doubted if he could find one elsewhere which he could do as easily. He read a great deal, he gardened, he did the crossword; he protected his property. At thirty-eight, it felt a bit like being retired already.

But when he met Ann — not that first moment at Repton Gardens, but later, after he'd conned himself into asking her out — he began to feel as if some long-broken line of communication to a self of twenty years ago had suddenly been restored. He felt once more capable of folly and idealism. He also felt as if his body had begun to exist again. By this he didn't just mean that he was seriously enjoying sex (though of course he did mean this too), but that he had stopped picturing himself as merely a brain lodged within a container. For at least ten years he had found a diminishing use for his body; the location of all pleasure and emotion, which had once seemed to extend right to the edge of his skin, had retreated to the small space in the middle of his head. Everything he valued went on between his ears. Of course, he looked after his body, but with the same sort of muted, impassive interest he showed towards his car. Both objects had to be fuelled and washed at varying intervals; both went wrong occasionally, but could usually be repaired.

893–8013: how had he found the nerve to make that call? He knew how: by fooling himself. He'd sat at his desk one morning with a list of phone calls and had slipped 'her' number into the middle of them. Halfway through rancorous haggling about timetables and resigned expressions of interest from editors of learned journals he found himself confronted by 'her' ringing tone. He hadn't asked anyone (any woman, that was) out to lunch (well, a non-professional lunch) for years. It had never seemed ... relevant. But all he had to do was identify himself, check that she remembered him, and ask away. She accepted; what's more, she said yes to the first day he suggested. He'd liked that; it had given him the confidence to leave his wedding ring on for the lunch. He had, for a moment, considered removing it.

And things had carried on as straightforwardly as that. He, or she, would say, 'Why don't we ... '; she, or he, would reply, 'Yes' or 'No'; and the decision was made. None of that speculation about motives which marriage to Barbara constantly involved. You didn't really mean that, Graham, did you? When you said $x$ you really meant $y$, didn't you, Graham? Living with you is like playing chess against someone with two ranks of knights, Graham. One evening in the seventh year of their marriage, after a dinner almost without tension, when Alice had gone to bed and he felt as soothed and happy as had seemed then to be possible, he had said to Barbara, exaggerating only a little,

'I feel very happy.'

And Barbara, who was scouring the final crumbs from the dinner-table, had wheeled round, pink rubber gloves wetly aloft, as if she were a poised surgeon, and answered,

'What are you trying to get out of?'

There had been similar exchanges, before and after, but this one stuck in his mind. Maybe because he really hadn't been trying to get out of anything. And afterwards, he found himself pausing before he told her he loved her, or was happy, or that things were going well, weren't they, and he'd first ponder the question: is there anything Barbara might think I'm trying to evade or diminish if I go ahead and tell her what I'm feeling? And if there wasn't, he'd go ahead and tell her. But it did take the spontaneity out of things.

Spontaneity, directness, the mending of communication lines to his body: Ann had introduced him not just to Pleasure (many might have done that) but to its intricate approaches, its mazy enjoyment; she even managed to freshen for him the memories of pleasure. The pattern of this introduction never varied: first, a thrust of recognition as he saw how Ann did something (ate, made love, talked, even just stood or walked); then, a period of mimetic catching-up, until he felt at ease in the presence of that particular pleasure; finally, a state of thankfulness edged (he didn't understand how it could be, at first, but it was) with queasy resentment. Grateful as he was to her for teaching him, approving as he did of her having found out first (without that, how could he ever have learnt?), he sometimes ran up against a residual, nervous vexation that Ann had got there before him. After all, he was seven years older than her. In bed, for instance, her confident easiness often seemed to him to be showing up (criticizing, mocking almost) his own cautious, stiff-jointed awkwardness. 'Hey, stop, wait for me,' he thought; and at other times, with more resentment, 'Why didn't you learn this with *me*?'

Ann was aware of this—she made Graham make her aware of it, as soon as she sensed it—but it didn't seem a threat. Talking would surely make it go away. Besides, there were many areas where Graham knew far more than she did.

History was a library of closed books to her. The news was uninteresting because it was inevitable, uninfluenceable. Politics bored her, except for the brief gambler's thrill she felt at Budget time, and the slightly more protracted thrill during general elections. She could just about name the important members of the Cabinet; except that she was normally one Cabinet behind.

She liked travelling, which Graham had almost given up (it was another activity which took place mainly between his ears). She liked modern art and old music; she hated sport and shopping; she loved food and reading. Graham found most of these tastes congenial, and all understandable. She used to like the cinema—she had, after all, had small parts in a number of films—but didn't want to go any more; which was fine by Graham.

When Ann met him she wasn't on the lookout. 'I'm thirty-one,' she had recently replied to an overconcerned uncle who stared pryingly at the third finger of her left hand, 'I'm not on the shelf, and I'm not on the lookout.' She no longer expected each party, each dinner to disclose a perfect partner—or even an adequate one. Besides, she had already grasped the baffling, comic disparity between intentions and results. You wanted a brief, almost contactless affair, and you got fond of his mother; you thought he was good but not wet, and discovered an adamantine selfishness behind his modest, drink-fetching appearance. Ann didn't consider herself disillusioned or (as some of her friends thought her) unlucky; she merely judged herself wiser than when she had started. So far, she thought, as she considered the uneasy *ménages à trois*, the tear-drenched abortions, and the niggling, low-grade relationships some of her friends let themselves in for, she'd got through pretty unscathed.

It was in Graham's favour that he wasn't particularly good-looking; Ann told herself it made him more authentic. Whether or not he was married was a neutral factor. Ann's girlfriends decreed that once you reached thirty, the men you met (unless you turned cradle-snatcher) tended to be either homosexual, married or psychotic, and that of the three, the married men were obviously the best. Sheila, Ann's closest friend, maintained that in any case married men were preferable to single men because they smelt nicer: their wives were always having their clothes dry-cleaned. Whereas the bachelor's jacket, she declared, was all cigarette smoke and armpits.

Ann's first affair with a married man had troubled her; she felt, if not exactly a thief, at least a white-collar criminal. But this didn't last long; and nowadays she argued that if marriages went stale, that was hardly her fault, was it? If men strayed, it was because they wanted to; if you took a principled stand, shoulder to shoulder with your fellow-woman, that wouldn't change anything. You wouldn't get any thanks for your negative virtue; the husband would soon move on to some tramp; and the wife would never know about your silent support. So, as she sat over lunch with Graham for the first time and noticed his wedding-ring, she only thought, Well, that gets me out of *that* question. It was always difficult when you had to ask. Sometimes they assumed you were wanting them to lie, and so they did, and then you were tempted into needlessly sarcastic comments like, 'You're terribly good at ironing.'

At the end of what was largely a dossier meal, Graham leaned towards her and in his nervousness failed to punctuate his two sentences:

'Will you have lunch with me again I'm married by the way.' She smiled and answered simply,

'Yes I will. Thank you for telling me.'

After the second lunch, with a little more to drink, he helped her into her coat more zealously, smoothing the material down over one shoulder blade as if the cloth had suddenly thrown up a ruckle. When Ann reported this to Sheila as being the full extent of their physical contact after three whole meetings, her friend commented,

'Maybe he's queer as well as married.' Whereupon Ann surprised herself by replying,

'It doesn't matter.'

It didn't. Or rather, it wouldn't have, she thought. But she duly found out, after an old-fashioned length of time (and after putting out enough signals to make a battle fleet alter course) that Graham wasn't homosexual. At first, they seemed to make love a bit as if it were socially expected; but gradually, they began to do so with what felt like the normal frequency, and with what felt like the normal motives. After three months Graham faked a conference in Nottingham, and they spent the weekend driving through smoke-blackened spa towns and sudden moorlands edged with drystone walls. Separately, they worried what might happen if Barbara phoned the hotel and discovered that she, Mrs Graham Hendrick, had already booked in. Separately, they decided that next time it would have to be two rooms and their own names.

Ann found herself surprised by the creeping realization that she was in love with Graham. He hadn't seemed at all an obvious candidate: he was eager and unco-ordinated, and kicked the legs of restaurant tables when he stood up to leave; whereas the men she had hitherto come closest to loving had been leisurely and relaxed. Graham was also what she supposed to be an intellectual; though she quickly discovered that he disliked talking about his work and seemed much more interested in hers. At first, the sight of him resetting his glasses on his nose as he bent over the special *prêt-à-porter* edition of French *Vogue* struck her as comical and vaguely threatening; but since, in reply, he showed no desire at all for her to accompany him to Colindale newspaper library and help collate the varying accounts of inter-war strikes and demonstrations, she began to stop worrying.

She felt, at the same time, both older and younger than him. Sometimes she pitied him for the narrowness of his previous life; at others she felt daunted by the thought that she would never know as many things as Graham, would never be able to argue with the directness and logic which she perceived in him. On occasions, lying in bed, she found herself thinking about his brain. Beneath that covering of patchily grey hair, how were the contents distinguishable from what lay beneath her own trimmed and sculpted (and lightly dyed) covering of blonde? Could you cut his head open and immediately notice a different structure? If he really *had* been a brain surgeon, perhaps he might have been able to tell her.

After their affair had lasted six months, it became necessary to tell Barbara. Necessary not for her but for them: they were taking too many risks; it would be better if they told her when *they* wanted to, rather than be forced to confess after a period of suspicion which would be painful for her and guilt-inducing for them. It would also be cleaner, easier for Barbara. That's what they told themselves. In addition, Graham hated having to go to the lavatory whenever he wanted to look at Ann's photograph.

Twice he funked it. The first time because Barbara was in one of her nicer moods and he couldn't bear to hurt her; the second because she was cheerfully hostile and he didn't want her to think he was merely telling her about Ann in revenge. He wanted the announcement to be unequivocal.

In the end, he could only do it the cowardly way: he stayed a whole night with Ann. It wasn't planned, but they fell asleep after making love, and when Ann roused him with a panicky slap he suddenly thought, Why should I? Why should I drive back through the cold just to lie next to a wife I don't love? So instead, he turned over, and let morally neutral sleep force his declaration.

By the time he got home Alice would normally have left for school; but she was still there.

'Daddy, I can go to school today, can't I?'

Graham hated moments like this. He turned towards Barbara, conscious that he would never again look at her in quite the same way, unchanging and unchangeable though she appeared: the short dark curls, the pouchily pretty face, the turquoise eyeliner. She was giving nothing away, and stared at him as expressionlessly as if he were a television newsreader.

'Um.' He looked again at Barbara; still no help. 'Um, I don't see why not.'

'We've got a history test today, Daddy.'

'Then you must go.'

Alice's answering smile never reached completion.

'Must? *Must*? What right have you to go about issuing *musts*? Come on, you tell me what right.' Barbara's anger turned a round face long, and soft features angular.

Graham hated moments like this even more. He was incompetent at arguing with Barbara; she always operated on such fearlessly non-academic principles. With his students he could argue quite well: calmly, logically, on a basis of agreed facts. At home, there was no such basis; you never seemed to start the discussion (or rather, the system of one-way reprimands) at the beginning, but splashed in at the middle; while the accusations he had to counter were a home weave of hypothesis, assertion, fantasy and malice. Worse still was the relentless emotional overlay to the argument: the threatened price of victory might be clattering hatred, haughty silence, or a meat cleaver in the back of the head.

'Alice, go to your room while your mother and I sort this out.'

'Why should she? Why shouldn't she hear about where your *musts* come from? Is that where you've been all night — out gathering *musts*? Come back with a nice set of orders for us, have you? Come on, tell me what my *musts* for the day are.'

Oh God, out of hand already.

'Is there something wrong with you, Alice?' he asked quietly. His daughter put her head down.

'No, Daddy.'

'She's had a nosebleed. I'm not sending a child to school with a nosebleed. Not at her age.'

There she went again. 'At her age' — what did that mean? Were there ages at which you could send daughters with nosebleeds to school? Or was Barbara merely pretending to draw on that Swiss bank account of 'feminine' reasons for doing or not doing things? Was it all related to that private mother–daughter domain from which Graham had been ritually excluded a couple of years earlier? Was 'nose-bleed' a euphemism?

'It's all right now.' Alice had lifted her face until her nostrils were pointing up towards her father. Even so, their insides were still in shadow; he didn't know whether he ought to bend down and examine them. He didn't know what to do.

'Alice, that's a disgusting habit,' Barbara announced, and roughly tapped her daughter's head down again. 'Go to your room and lie down, and if you feel better in an hour I'll let you go to school with a note.'

Graham realized his ineptness at this sort of squabbling. In one move, Barbara had reasserted her authority over their daughter, ensured that she would remain in the house as a distant witness to her delinquent father's trial, and established herself as Alice's future liberator, thus securing the continued alliance against Graham. How did she do it?

'Well,' Barbara stated rather than asked, before (though only just before) Alice closed the kitchen door. Graham didn't reply; he was listening for Alice's footsteps on the stairs. But all he heard was,

'WEEEEEEEEEEEELLLLLLLL.'

' . . . '

The only technique Graham had taught himself in fifteen years was to allow the first few dozen accusations to declare themselves before he joined in.

'Graham, what do you mean by staying out all night and not letting me know and coming home at this hour and trying to run my house for me?'

That was four to start with. Graham already felt he was beginning to detach himself from the house, from Barbara, even from Alice. And if Barbara needed to play complicated games to secure Alice's sympathy, then clearly she needed the girl more than he did.

'I'm having an affair. I'm leaving you.'

Barbara looked at him as if she didn't recognize him. He had stopped being even the newsreader; he had become almost a burglar. She didn't say a word. He felt it was his turn to speak, but there wasn't much to add.

''Im having an affair. I don't love you any more. I'm leaving you.'

'You're not. I'll see to it. If you try, I'll get on to ... to the university authorities.'

Of course, she would think that. She would think that the only person he could possibly be having an affair with was a student. That was how limited she thought he was. This realization gave him more confidence.

'It's not a student. I'm leaving you.'

Barbara screamed, very loudly, and Graham didn't believe her. When she stopped, he merely said,

'I think you've probably got Alice on your side anyway, without all that.'

Barbara screamed again, just as loud, and for just as long. Graham felt unmoved, almost cocky. He wanted to leave; he was going to leave; he was going to love Ann. No, he did love Ann already. He was going to go on loving Ann.

'Careful—it might get counterproductive. I'm going to work now.'

That day he taught three classes on Baldwin without feeling any tedium at either his own repetitions or his students' well-meant banalities. He phoned Ann to tell her to expect him that evening. At lunchtime he bought a large suitcase, a fresh tube of toothpaste, some dental floss, and a flannel as furry as a bearskin rug. He felt as if he were going on holiday. Yes, it would be a holiday, a long, unending holiday

—what's more, with holidays within the holiday. The thought made him feel silly. He went back to the chemist's and bought a roll of film.

He got home at five o'clock and went straight upstairs without looking for his wife or daughter. From the telephone extension by the bed he made a call to the local taxi service. As he was putting down the phone, Barbara walked into the bedroom. He didn't speak to her, but merely opened his new suitcase flat on the bed. They both looked inside it; the Kodak film carton glared back at them, raucously orange.

'You're not taking the car.'

'I'm not taking the car.'

'You're not taking anything.'

'I'm not taking anything.'

'You take everything, *everything*, do you hear?' Graham carried on filling the suitcase with clothes.

'I want the front door keys.'

'You can have them.'

'I'm changing the locks.' (Then why ask for the keys, Graham wondered half-heartedly.)

Barbara went away. Graham finished packing his clothes, his razor, a photograph of his parents, one of his daughter, then started to close the case. It was only half-full. All that he wanted was less than a caseload. He felt exhilarated at the discovery, lightened by it. He had once read a biography of Aldous Huxley, and remembered being puzzled by the writer's behaviour when his house in Hollywood was burnt down. Huxley had meekly watched it happen: his manuscripts, his notebooks, his entire library were destroyed without interference from their owner. There was lots of time, but all he chose to save were three suits and a violin. Graham now felt he understood. Three suits and a violin. He looked down at his case and was slightly ashamed of its size.

As he picked it up he heard the clothes fall softly towards the hinges; they would be crumpled by the time he arrived.

He put the case in the hall and went into the kitchen; Barbara was sitting at the table. He placed in front of her his car keys and his house keys. In reply she pushed towards him a large plastic laundry bag.

'Don't imagine I'm doing *this* for you.'

He nodded and picked up the bag.

'I'd better say goodbye to Alice.'

'She's staying with a friend. She's staying the night. I said she could. *Like you did,*' Barbara added, though it sounded weary rather than venomous.

'Which friend?'

Barbara didn't reply. Graham nodded again and left. With his case in his right hand and his washing in his left, he walked down the front path, along Wayton Drive, and turned into Highfield Grove. That was where he'd asked the taxi to wait. He didn't want to embarrass Barbara (maybe he even thought to gain a squirt of sympathy by leaving on foot); but he was damned if he was going to arrive at Ann's, arrive for Part Two of his life, by public transport.

The taxi-driver inspected Graham and his luggage without comment. Graham thought it must look like some botched midnight flit, which had either gone off too soon or fallen pathetically behind schedule. But he felt confident enough not to explain, and hummed to himself in the back of the taxi. After a mile or so he spotted on the verge a slatted wooden rubbish bin, told the driver to stop, and dumped his laundry. You didn't arrive for the honey time with a bag of dirty washing.

And so the unending holiday began. Graham and Ann spent six months in her flat before finding a small terraced house with a garden in Clapham. Barbara proved yet again her capacity to wrong-foot Graham by insisting on a divorce at once. None of that blame-free two-year-separation stuff either: she wanted a proper, old-fashioned fault divorce. In the face of her demands Graham remained as passive as Huxley. He would continue to pay the mortgage; he would pay an allowance for Alice; Barbara could keep the car and the entire contents of the house. She would accept no money specifically for her own support; she would only accept it indirectly. She intended taking a job. Graham, and later the court, found these proposals fair.

The decree nisi came through in the late summer of 1978; Graham was granted weekly access to Alice. Shortly afterwards, he and Ann were married. They spent their honeymoon on Naxos, in a small whitewashed house owned by one of Graham's colleagues. They did everything normal to those in their position—made love frequently, drank quantities of Samian wine, gazed longer than necessary at the octopuses drying on the harbour wall—yet Graham felt curiously unmarried. He felt happy, but he didn't feel married.

After a fortnight they took a boat full of livestock and widows back to Piraeus, then another full of pensioners and academics up the Adriatic coast to Venice; five days later they flew home. As the plane crossed the Alps, Graham held the hand of his neat, kind, unimprovable wife, and repeated softly to himself that he was a happy man. This had been the holiday within the holiday; now the outer holiday would resume. There seemed no reason for any of it ever to end.

And as the next two years unfolded, Graham duly began to feel married. Perhaps subconsciously he'd been expecting it to be the same as the first time round. Marrying Barbara had involved an urgent if sometimes unco-ordinated erotic spree, a hurtling thrill at the novelty of love, and a distant sense of duty fulfilled towards parents and society. This time, the emphases were different: he and Ann had already been sleeping together for over a year; love the second time round made him wary rather than drunk; and certain friends were grumpy and distant with him over his abandonment of Barbara. Others expressed caution: once bitten, twice bitten, they warned.

What happened to make Graham feel married was that

nothing happened: nothing to stir fear or distrust at his condition, at life's treatment of him. And so, gradually, his feelings billowed out like a parachute, and after that alarming initial descent, everything suddenly slowed down, and he hung there, the sun on his face, the ground scarcely moving towards him. He felt, not so much that Ann represented his last chance, but that she had always represented his first and only chance. This is what they meant, he thought; now I see.

As his easiness in the face of love grew, his fascination with it—and with Ann—intensified. Things felt, paradoxically, both more solid and more precarious. Whenever Ann was away on business, he found that he missed her not sexually, but morally. When she wasn't there he shrank, he bored himself, he became stupider and a little frightened; he felt unworthy of her, and a suitable husband only for Barbara. And when Ann returned, he found himself watching her, studying her far more closely than he had done when they had first met. Sometimes this meticulous passion became desperate and driven. He envied the things she touched. He was contemptuous of the years he had spent without her. He felt frustrated at not being allowed to *be* her, not even for a day. Instead, he conducted interior duologues, one part of him acting Ann while another part acted himself. He confirmed from these conversations that they really did get on extraordinarily well. He didn't tell Ann about this habit—didn't want to burden her with too many specifics of his love, in case ... well, in case the details embarrassed her; in case he seemed to be asking for reciprocation.

He often imagined himself explaining his life to passers-by —to anyone, really, who was interested enough to ask. No one ever did ask, but that was probably more out of politeness than lack of interest. Even so, Graham had his answers ready just in case, and he would recite them to himself every so often, telling his whispered rosary of surprised joy. Ann had made the spectrum wider for him, had restored to him those lost colours everyone had the right to see. How long had he been managing on green and blue and indigo? Now he saw more, and he felt safe; existentially safe. One thought recurred like a bass figure in his new life, and brought him strange comfort. At least now, he would say to himself, now that I've got Ann, at least now I'll be properly mourned.

# TWO

## *In flagrante*

He ought, of course, to have suspected something earlier. After all, Barbara knew that he hated the cinema. He hated it; she hated it: this had been one of their first courting bonds, twenty years ago. They had politely sat through *Spartacus*, occasionally rubbing elbows in a fashion denoting awkwardness rather than desire, and had afterwards separately confessed that not only hadn't they enjoyed the film, but they hadn't much valued the underlying concept either. Not going to the cinema had been one of their first observable characteristics as a couple.

And now, according to Barbara, their daughter wanted him to take her to a film. He suddenly realized that he hadn't the slightest idea whether or not Alice had ever seen one before. She must have done, of course—unless her genetic inheritance in the area of aesthetics was abnormally domineering. But he didn't actually know. This made him sad. Three years away and you didn't know the simplest things. And then it made him sadder. Three years away and you didn't even ask yourself whether or not you knew.

But why did Alice want to go with him—and why to a re-run of a five-year-old British-made comedy flop at the Holloway Odeon?

'Apparently there's a scene in it which was filmed at her school,' came Barbara's offhand reply down the phone; his daughter's request, as usual, was not being communicated to him directly. 'All her friends are going.'

'Can't she go with them?'

'I think she's still a bit frightened of cinemas. I think she'd be happier with a grown-up.' Not with you as you; just with you as a grown-up.

Graham agreed; he usually did nowadays.

When he got to the Odeon with Alice the wisdom of his two decades' abstention was confirmed. The foyer smelt of softly frying onions, which patrons were encouraged to smear on hot dogs to ward off the chill of a warm July afternoon. Their tickets, he noted, cost as much as a shoulder of lamb. Inside, despite the scarcity of customers, the auditorium was murky with cigarette smoke. No doubt because the few who were there kept on lighting two cigarettes for themselves at the same time, in craven imitation of whatever that American film was that Graham had resolutely not seen.

When the flick started (Graham used the limiting noun of his adolescence: 'movie' was American, and 'film' made him think of 'film studies'), he remembered a lot more about why he didn't like the cinema. People talked about the artificiality of opera; but had they ever looked at this stuff properly? Garish colours, ludicrous plot, 1880s music with a topping of Copland, and the moral complication of a copy of the *Dandy*. Of course, *Over the Moon* was probably a poor example of the genre; but then it was always bad art that one examined to get the clearest idea of the form's basic conventions.

Meanwhile, whoever thought that a comedy-thriller about a very fat burglar who kept getting stuck in coal-holes was a good idea? And who then topped it by coming up with a thin detective whose gammy leg made him run even more slowly than the fat burglar? Oh look, said Graham to himself as one of the chase-scenes was suddenly speeded up against a background of honky-tonk piano, they've discovered *that* technique. More dismaying still was the fact that the two dozen people in the audience—none of whom appeared to go to Alice's school—seemed to be laughing quite genuinely. He felt his daughter tug on his sleeve.

'Daddy, has something gone wrong with the film?'

'Yes, darling, the projector's on the blink,' he replied; adding, when the scene finished, 'It's mended now.'

From time to time he squinted across at Alice, fearful that she would be excited by the cinema—the child of teetotal parents swilling a tot of sweet sherry. Yet her face stayed expressionless except for a slight frown, which Graham knew was her way of registering contempt. He waited for the scene featuring her school, but much of the action was indoors; during one long-shot of a city which was meant to be Birmingham (but which Graham judged to be London) he thought he spotted a familiar building in the mid-distance.

'Is that it?'

But Alice merely frowned more fiercely, bullying her father into shamed silence.

After about an hour, the trail of the obese housebreaker led the handicapped sleuth quite by chance to a much grander villain, an Italianate, lightly-moustached club-chair loller who acted contempt for the law by pulling slowly on a cheroot. The damaged detective at once started opening all the doors of the flat. In the bedroom he found Graham's wife. She was wearing dark glasses and reading a book; the sheets were chastely swaddled round her breasts, but the implications of the rumpled bed were clear. No wonder the film received an A certificate.

As the hero suddenly recognized an apparently well-known beauty queen, and as Graham recognized his viciously peroxided wife, she said, in a voice deep enough to be dubbed,

'I don't want any publicity.'

Graham let out a violent chuckle, obliterating for himself the reply of the calipered gumshoe. He glanced across at Alice and noted the return of her shaming frown.

During the two-minute scene that followed, Graham's second wife acted in turn surprise, anger, contempt, doubt, puzzlement, contrition, panic and, a second time round, anger. It was the emotional equivalent of a speeded-up chase. She also had time to reach across towards the telephone on the bedside table, thus giving those among the twenty-six people in the Holloway Odeon whose vision was not diminished by smoking two cigarettes at the same time a brief glimpse of her bare shoulders. Then she vanished from the screen, as well, doubtless, as from the mind of every casting director who had been unable to avoid seeing the film.

When they came out, Graham was still smiling to himself.

'Was that it?' he asked Alice.

'Was what what?' she replied with pedantic seriousness. At least she got something of her character from him.

'Was that the school in that shot?'

'What school?'

'*Your* school, of course.'

'What makes you think it was my school?'

Ah. Uh-huh.

'I thought that was why we went to the film, Alice: because you wanted to see your school.'

'No.' Again, a frown.

'Haven't all your friends been going to see it this week?'

'No.'

Ah well, no, of course not.

'What did you think of the film?'

'I thought it was a waste of time and money. It didn't even go anywhere interesting, like Africa. The only funny bit was when the projector went wrong.'

Fair enough. They got into Graham's car and drove carefully up to Alice's favourite teashop in Highgate. He knew it was Alice's favourite, because in three years of taking her out on Sunday afternoons they'd tried every teashop in North London. As usual, they had chocolate eclairs. Graham ate with his fingers; Alice with a fork. Neither of them commented on this, nor on any of the other ways in which she was growing into a person marked off from the one she might have been if he hadn't left home. Graham didn't think it fair to mention such things, and hoped she didn't notice them herself. She did notice every one of them, of course; but had been taught by Barbara that it was bad manners to point out other people's bad manners to them.

After dabbing her lips with a napkin—Don't be a Human Blowpipe, her mother always said—she remarked neutrally,

'Mummy told me you specially wanted to see that film.'

'Oh, did she? Did she say why?'

'She said you wanted to see Ann in one of ... what was it ... "her most convincing screen roles", I think that's what she said.' Alice was looking at him solemnly. Graham felt cross; but there was no point in taking it out on Alice.

'I think that might have been one of Mummy's jokes,' he said. One of her cleverer ones, too. 'I tell you what. Why don't we have a joke back on Mummy? Why don't we say we tried to get in to *Over the Moon*, but it was packed out, so we had to go and see the new James Bond instead?' He supposed there was a new James Bond; there usually seemed to be.

'All right.' Alice smiled, and Graham thought, She does take after me, yes she does. But maybe he only thought that when she agreed with him. They sipped at their tea for a while; then she said,

'It wasn't a very good film, was it, Daddy?'

'No, I'm afraid it wasn't.' Another pause. Then he added, uncertainly, but sensing the question was being invited, 'What did you think of Ann?'

'I thought she was *rubbish*,' Alice replied vehemently. She did take after Barbara; he'd got it wrong. 'She was such a ... such a *tart*.'

Graham, as always, concealed his reaction to her lexical discoveries.

33

'She was only acting.' But he sounded conciliatory rather than sage.

'Well, I just think she did it too darn well.'

Graham looked across at the open, pleasant, but still unformed face of his daughter. Which way would it jump, he wondered: into that odd combination of sharpness and pudginess he now associated with Barbara, or into a thoughtful, tolerant, mellow elongation? For her sake, he hoped she would resemble neither of her parents.

They finished their tea, and Graham drove her even more slowly than usual back to Barbara's house. That was how he thought of it nowadays. He used to think of it as their house; now it was just Barbara's. And it didn't even have the decency to look different. Graham felt resentful towards the house for not getting itself repainted or something, for not committing some act symbolic of its new, single ownership. But the house was clearly on Barbara's side. It always had been, he supposed. Every week its sameness was intended to remind him of his ... what, treachery?

Perhaps; though Barbara's sense of betrayal wasn't as sharp as she let him continue to believe. She had always been a Marxist about emotions, believing that they shouldn't just exist for themselves, but should do some work if they were to eat. Besides, she had for some years been more interested in her daughter and her house than in her husband. People expected her to cry thief, and she did so; but she didn't always believe herself.

It was the last Sunday of the month: as usual, Barbara let Alice slip in under her elbow and then handed Graham an envelope. It contained details of the month's additional expenses for which she judged him liable. Occasionally it would be a bill for some reckless treat which Barbara held to be necessary if Alice was ever to overcome the unmappable hurt of Graham's departure; the claim was unanswerable, his cheque wry.

Graham stuffed the envelope into his pocket without

comment. Normally he replied with another silently-accepted envelope the following Sunday. Queries were dealt with on Thursday evenings, when he rang up and was allowed to talk to Alice for between five and ten minutes, depending on her mother's mood.

'Enjoy the film?' Barbara enquired levelly. She was looking neat and pretty, her tight dark curls newly washed. It was her going-out-and-having-a-good-time-and-stuff-you look; as opposed to her martyred-by-housework-and-being-a-single-parent-and-stuff-you look. Graham felt roughly the same indifference towards both guises. He felt a complacent lack of curiosity about why he had ever loved her in the first place. That black hair, inhumanly flawless in colour; that round, forgettable face; those guilt-inducing eyes.

'Couldn't get in,' he replied, just as levelly. 'It's one of those cinemas they've split up into three, and I suppose all her schoolfriends had got there before us.'

'So what did you do?'

'Oh, well, we thought, once we were there, we might as well see something, so we went to the new James Bond instead.'

'What EVER for?' Her tone was sharper, more rebuking than he could have predicted. 'You'll give the child nightmares. *Really*, Graham.'

'I think she's too sensible for that.'

'Well, all I can say is, on your head be it. On *your head*.'

'Yes. Yes, okay then. See you ... talk to you on Thursday.' He backed off the doorstep like a rebuffed brush salesman.

Even the jokes turned sour with Barbara nowadays. She'd find out in due course that they hadn't been to the Bond film — Alice would keep it up for a bit and then crack, in that rather solemn way of hers — but by then Barbara would be past seeing it as a simple revenge joke. Why did she always do this to him? Why did he always feel like this when driving away? Oh, stuff it, he thought. Stuff it.

'Good visit?'

'Not bad.'

'Cost much?' Ann wasn't referring to the direct price of taking Alice out, but to the indirect one, the one in the sealed envelope. And perhaps to other indirect costs as well.

'Haven't looked.' He tossed the monthly reckoning on to the coffee table unopened. He always felt depressed returning from the failed part of his life to the active one; that was inevitable, he supposed. And he always underestimated Barbara's talent for making him feel like a bob-a-job boy: the envelope, he suspected, might as well contain his signed cub's card, while even now his ex-wife would be putting up the 'Job Done' sticker with its big red tick.

He went through to the kitchen, where Ann was already pouring him a half-and-half gin-and-tonic, her usual prescription for him at this time of the week.

'Nearly caught you *in flagrante*,' he said smilingly.

'Eh?'

'Nearly caught you, today, *in flagrante* with the other fellow,' he expatiated.

'Ah. Which of them?' She hadn't located the joke yet.

'That Eyetie fellow. Thin moustache, velvet smoking jacket, cheroot, glass of champagne in the hand—that one.'

'Ah. That one.' She was still puzzled. 'Enrico or Antonio? They both have thin moustaches and swill champagne all the time.'

'Riccardo.'

'Oh, Riccardo.' Come on, Graham, get to the point, she thought. Stop making me feel nervous.

'Riccardo Devlin.'

'Devlin … Christ, Dick Devlin. Oh, you don't mean you saw *Over the Moon*? … God, wasn't it awful? Wasn't *I* awful?'

'Just bad casting. And they didn't have Faulkner on the script, did they?'

'I sat there in bed, wearing ridiculous dark glasses, and said, "I don't want any of this to come out"—or something like that. Star part.'

'That might have been an improvement. No, it was, "I don't want any publicity".'

'Well, I certainly didn't get any; quite right too. *And* I got punished for being a loose woman.'

'Mmmm.'

'What did you see *that* for? I thought you were going to some film with Alice's school in.'

'We were. Except that I doubt if such a film really exists. It was ... well, I suppose it was one of Barbara's jokes.'

'Fucking Barbara. Fucking Barbara.'

'Oh, I wouldn't say that, love.'

'No, really—fucking Barbara. You get three hours a week with that kid and that's all, and *she* uses it to get back at me.'

'I shouldn't think that was her motive.' He didn't mean it.

'What else could it have been? She just wanted you to see me acting badly, and get you embarrassed in front of Alice. You know how suggestible kids are. Now Alice'll just think of me as a screen whore.'

'She's much too sensible for that.'

'No one is at her age. That's what I look like in the film; that's what she'll think. "Daddy's gone and married a scrubber," she'll say to her friends at school tomorrow. Your daddies are all married to your mummies, but *my* Daddy's gone off and left Mummy and married a scrubber. I saw her on Sunday. A real *scrubber*." ' Ann mimicked girlish horror.

'No she won't. Shouldn't think she knows the word anyway,' Graham replied, without convincing himself.

'Well, it's bound to make an impact, isn't it? Fucking Barbara,' she repeated, this time as a summing-up.

Graham still got a mild shock when he heard Ann swear. He always remembered the first time it had happened. They'd been walking along the Strand on a rainy evening, when all of a sudden she'd let go of his arm, stopped, looked down at the backs of her legs and said, 'Fuck'. She (or, for all he knew, he) had splashed some dirty water on to her calf. Only one calf; that was all. It would wash out of her tights; it didn't hurt; it was dark, so no one would notice; and they were at the end, not the beginning, of the evening. But even so, she had said 'Fuck'. It had been a nice evening; they'd had a good dinner together, got on well, hadn't run short of things to say; but even so, a couple of drops of water and it brought out a 'Fuck'. What on earth would she say if something serious happened? If she broke a leg or the Russians landed?

Barbara had never sworn. Graham had never sworn when he was with Barbara. Nothing beyond 'Damn', anyway; except to himself. That evening, as he and Ann continued along the Strand, he enquired mildly,

'What would you say if the Russians landed?'

'Eh? Is that a threat or a promise?'

'No, I mean, you just swore when you splashed your tights. I wondered what you'd say if you broke your leg or the Russians landed or something.'

'Graham,' she replied carefully, 'I think I'll cross that bridge when I get to it.'

They had walked on in silence for a bit.

'I suppose you think I'm being priggish. I only wanted to know.'

'Let's say, perhaps you've led a rather sheltered life.'

They had left it at that for the time being; and Graham couldn't help noticing how, as he got closer to Ann, he began to swear more himself. At first hesitantly, then with relief, then with expansive relish. Now he swore automatically, as mere punctuation, like everyone else. He assumed that if and when the Russians came, then the right words would come too.

'What was it like, making *Over the Moon*?' he asked Ann as they were washing up together that evening.

'Oh, a bit less fun than some. Lots of studio work. Low budget, so we all had to wear the same clothes a lot. I remember they chopped around the script and made several scenes happen on the same day, just so that we wouldn't have too many changes.'

'And how was your Italian inamorato?'

'Dick Devlin? He was as English as the East End. Hasn't exactly made it into lights so far, has he? In fact, I *think* I saw him doing a shaving commercial a few weeks ago. He was nice; not much talent, but nice. Couldn't act, just used what he called his "glower power". Took me bowling one afternoon when they didn't need us. Bowling!'

'And ... ' Graham, who had been drying, turned away and started folding napkins, so that when Ann answered she wouldn't be able to catch his eye. ' ... did you?'

'Oh yes.' From the direction of her voice he knew she was looking at him. 'Just once, I think.'

'No more than a sneeze.'

'Not much.'

Graham patted the napkins flat, picked up a teaspoon that didn't need washing, carried it over to the sink and slipped it into the water. As he did so, he kissed Ann on the side of the neck and made a little sneezing noise. Then he kissed her again, in the same place.

He liked the way she answered him directly. She was never coy, or sly, or evasive. She never took the line, which she justifiably might, of 'You haven't earned the knowledge'. She just told him, and that was that. He liked it this way: if he asked, he got told; if he didn't ask, he didn't get told. Simple. He picked up the coffee tray and wandered off to the sitting-room.

Ann was glad she'd got out of acting when she had — which was a few months before she met Graham. Eight years was quite enough for her to realize the random correlation that existed between talent and employment. A variety of stage, television and, latterly, film work, had convinced her that at her best she was really quite good; which was precisely not good enough for her.

She had wrangled with herself for some months and finally

39

got out. Not out into resting, but out into something full-time and different, by cleverly using Nick Slater's friendship to ease her into Redman and Gilks. (It had been clever not only not to sleep with him before he made the offer, but to make it clear that even if he did give her the job she still wouldn't. He had seemed relieved, almost respectful, when faced with such intransigence. Perhaps that was the best way, she thought later, the modern way: nowadays you get jobs by not sleeping with people.) And it had worked out. Within three years she was deputy chief buyer, with a six-figure budget, as much travel as she wanted, and hours which, though sometimes long, were determined by her own efficiency. She had sensed an unfamiliar stability entering her life even before she met Graham; now, things felt solider than ever.

On the Thursday Graham rang Barbara and haggled briefly about the bills.

'But why does she need so many clothes?'

'Because she needs them.' (The classic Barbara answer: take a chunk of your sentence and simply repeat it. Less work for her, plus time saved for preparing the next answer but one.)

'Why does she need three bras?'

'She needs them.'

'Why? Does she wear them all at once—one on top of the other?'

'One on, one clean, and one in the wash.'

'But I paid for three only a few months ago.'

'You may not have noticed, Graham, and I doubt if you care, but your daughter's growing. She's changing ... size.'

He wanted to say, 'Oh, you mean she's busting out all over'; but he no longer had confidence in jokes with Barbara. Instead he quibbled mildly.

'She's growing that fast?'

'Graham, if you constrict a growing girl, there is untold damage that can be done. Bind up the body and you affect

the mind; it's well known. I really didn't know your mean-
ness went as far as that.'

He hated these conversations; not least because he
suspected that Barbara half-invited Alice to listen in and
then rouged her side of the argument accordingly.

'Fine. Okay. Fine. Oh, and by the way, thanks for the
delayed wedding present, if that's what it was.'

'The what?'

'The wedding present. I take it that's what Sunday afternoon was.'

'Ah. Yes; glad you liked it.' For once, she sounded a bit
defensive, so he instinctively pushed again.

'Though I really can't imagine why you did it.'

'Can't you? Can't you imagine?'

'No, I mean, why you should be interested ... '

'Oh, I just think you ought to know what you've let
yourself in for.' Her tone was precise and maternal; he felt
his position slipping.

'Nice of you.' Bitch, he added to himself.

'Don't mention it. And I think it's important for Alice to
see the sort of influence her father's currently under.' He
didn't miss that *currently*.

'But how did you find out Ann was in it? She isn't exactly
on the poster.'

'I have my spies, Graham.'

'Come on, how did you find out?' But all she would say
was,

'I have my spies.'

# THREE

## *The Cross-Eyed Bear*

Jack Lupton answered the door with a smouldering cigarette lodged in the side of his beard. He stretched his arms out, pulled Graham in, dropped a hand on his shoulder, belted him on the bottom, and finally propelled him down the hall bellowing,

'Graham, you old cunt, in you go.'

Graham couldn't help smiling. A lot of Jack was bullshit, he suspected, and that lot came under regular analysis among his friends; but in person he was so uncompromisingly amiable, so noisily open and so physical that you immediately forgot the precise terms of yesterday's derision. The matiness may have been assumed, part of an act to make you like him; but if so, it worked, and as it continued without hesitation or change of key—in Graham's case, for five or six years—you ended up not needing to worry about its sincerity.

The cigarette trick had started as a joky short-cut to character. Jack's beard grew wirily enough for him to park a Gauloise in it safely, at a point halfway along the jawbone. If he was chatting up a girl at a party, he'd go off to fetch some drinks and free his hands by tucking his lighted cigarette into his beard (sometimes he would light one specially to set up the effect). On his return, a chunky blur of bonhomie, he'd adopt one of three courses, depending on his appraisal of the girl. If she seemed sophisticated, or acute, or even just alert, he'd casually extract the cigarette and go on smoking (this established him, he assured Graham, as 'a bit of an original'). If she seemed dim or shy or charmproof, he'd leave the cigarette there for a minute or two, talk about a book—though never one of his own—and then ask for a smoke (this proved him to be 'one of those clever, absent-minded writers with his head in the clouds'). If he couldn't fathom her at all, or thought she was crazy, or was quite drunk himself, he'd simply leave the cigarette until it smouldered its way down to his beard, then look puzzled and ask, 'Can you smell something burning around here?' (this established him as 'really a terrific character, a bit wild, probably a bit self-destructive, you know, like real artists, but *so* interesting'). When using this third ploy, he would normally accompany it with some serpentine inventions about his childhood or his ancestry. It did, however, have its dangers. He'd once inflicted a bad burn on himself in pursuit of an attractive but strangely enigmatic girl. He couldn't imagine she hadn't noticed the cigarette, and his rising incredulity paralleled his increasing pain; later, he discovered that while he'd been off fetching them drinks the girl had taken out her contact lenses: the smoke from his cigarette had been irritating her eyes.

'Coffee?' Jack bashed Graham on the shoulder again.

'Please.'

The ground floor of Jack's Repton Gardens flat had been knocked through, from front bay to back kitchen; they were sitting in the crepuscular middle section, which Jack used as a living room. In the bay stood his desk, with a piano stool in front of it; his electric typewriter was barely visible beneath the contents of an upturned litter bin. Jack had once explained to Graham his theory of creative chaos. He was by nature a very tidy person, he claimed, but his art demanded mess. The words simply refused to flow, apparently, unless they sensed that there was some sexy anarchy out there on which their ordered form could make an impact. Hence the litter of paper, magazines, brown envelopes and last season's pools coupons. 'They need to feel there's some point in being born,' Jack had explained. 'It's like those aboriginal tribes where the women parturate on to piles of old newspapers. Same principle. Same newspapers, probably.'

As Jack took his chunky form off to the kitchen extension he pivoted slightly on one leg and farted, quite loudly.

'Not I, But the Wind,' he muttered, almost to himself, but not quite.

Graham had heard that one before. He'd heard most of them before; but didn't really mind. As Jack had gradually become a better-known novelist, as his fame permitted him self-indulgence and eccentricity, he'd taken to farting quite a lot. Nor were they the embarrassed exhalations of a senescent sphincter; they were rowdy, worked-at, middle-aged farts. Somehow—Graham didn't even understand the process—Jack had made it into an acceptable mannerism.

And it wasn't just that he made it acceptable once it had happened. Graham sometimes thought he planned it. Once, Jack had rung up and insisted that he help him choose a squash racquet. Graham protested that he'd only ever played squash three times—once with Jack, when he'd been sent scurrying around the court towards a heart attack—but Jack refused to accept his disclaimers of authority. They met in the sports department of Selfridges, and though Graham could quite plainly see the squash and tennis racquets over to their left, Jack had dragged him off on a tour of the whole floor. After about ten yards, though, he suddenly stopped, did his pre-fart pivot so that his back was towards a slanting row of cricket bats, and sounded off. As they walked on, he muttered sideways to Graham,

'The Wind in the Willows.'

Five minutes later, when Jack had decided that maybe after all he'd stick with the racquet he'd got, Graham wondered if it hadn't all been planned that way; if Jack hadn't simply found himself with time and a joke on his hands, and telephoned Graham to help him get rid of both.

'Okay, boyo.' Jack (who wasn't Welsh) handed Graham a mug of coffee, sat down, took a sip of his own, plucked the cigarette from his beard and puffed on it. 'Sympathetic novelist lends sensitive ear to worried academic. Fifteen pounds —make that guineas—per hour; unlimited sessions. And make it something I can, with all my transformational powers, turn into a two hundred quid story minimum, and that's my little joke. Shoot.'

Graham fiddled with his glasses for a few seconds; then took a sip of coffee. Too soon: he felt some taste-buds getting burned out by the heat. He wrapped his hands round the mug and stared into it.

'It's not that I want you to give me specific advice. It's not that I want you to confirm to me a certain line of action that I'm too timid to adopt without a second opinion. I'm just worried, I sort of can't get over how I'm reacting to … to what it is I'm reacting to. I, well, I didn't know about this sort of thing. And I thought, Jack's got more experience of the whole caboodle than I have, may even have had attacks of it himself, probably knows someone who has, anyway.'

Graham looked up towards Jack, but the steam from the coffee had misted his glasses; he saw only a brownish blur.

'Old matey, you're about as clear as a bugger's back passage so far.'

'Ah, sorry. Jealousy,' Graham said suddenly. Then, trying to be helpful, 'Sexual jealousy.'

'No other kind in my experience. Hmmm. Sorry to hear it, old darling. The little lady been playing with fire, has she?' Jack wondered why on earth Graham had come to him—him of all people. His tone became even more familiar. 'Never can tell, that's what I say. Never can tell what you've got until it's too late, and by then it's tweezers round your tassle.' He waited for Graham to continue.

'No, it's not that. Good God, that would be awful. Awful. No, it's sort of … retrospective, it's all retrospective. It's all about chaps before me. Before she met me.'

45

'Ah.' Jack became more alert; and more puzzled still why Graham had come to him.

'Went to a film the other day. Crappy film. Ann was in it. Some other fellow — won't tell you his name — was in it too, and later it came out that Ann was, had, had been to bed with him. Not much,' Graham added quickly, 'once or twice. Didn't — you know — didn't *go out* with him or anything.'

'Mm.'

'I went back to see that film three times in one week. The first time I thought, you know, interesting to have another look at the fellow's face: I hadn't really paid him that much attention the first time. So I had another look, and I didn't like the face much, but then I wouldn't, would I? And then I found myself going back again, twice more. It wasn't even a local cinema, it was up in Holloway. I even rearranged a class one day so that I could get out to it.'

'And — and what was it like?'

'Well, the first time — that's to say the second time altogether — it was ... funny as much as anything. The ... bloke was acting some sort of minor mafia person, but I knew — Ann had told me — that he came from the East End, so I was listening carefully, and he couldn't even sustain the accent for more than three words in a row. And I thought, why couldn't Ann have gone to bed with a better actor? And I sort of laughed at him, and I thought, well, I may not be Casanova, but I'm a sodding better academic than you'll *ever* be a good actor. And I remembered Ann saying she thought he'd been doing shaving commercials lately, and I thought, poor sod; maybe that film was the high point of his professional career and he's all twisted up with failure and envy and guilt and occasionally he's standing in the dole queue and he finds himself thinking wistfully about Ann and what's become of her, and when I came out of the cinema I thought, "Well, stuff *you*, matey, *stuff you*."

'The second time — the third time — I suppose that was the

puzzle. Why did I go back then? I just did. I felt I ... ought to. I felt I had a hunch: a hunch about myself, that's all I can say. I was probably in a funny mood, and I couldn't work out why I was in the cinema anyway—this was when I'd rearranged the class —and I sat through the incredibly boring first half hour or so, and I wasn't sure what I was going to feel but somehow I knew it wasn't going to be the same as before. I suppose I should have left then.'

'Why didn't you?'

'Oh, some childhood puritanism about getting my money's worth.' Actually, that wasn't right. 'No, it was more than that. I tell you what I think it was: it was feeling I was near something dangerous. It was the expectation of not knowing what to expect. Does that sound—cerebral?'

'A bit.'

'Well it wasn't. It was very physical in fact. I was trembling. I felt I was going to be let into a great secret. I felt I was going to be frightened. I felt like a child.'

There was a pause. Graham slurped at his coffee.

'And were you frightened? Tumble-drier tum-tum?'

'Sort of. It's hard to explain. I wasn't frightened *of* this fellow, I was frightened *about* him. I felt very aggressive, but in a completely unspecific way. I also felt I was going to be sick, but that was something separate, extra. I was very ... upset, I suppose I'd say.'

'Sounds like it. What about the last time?'

'Same again. Same reactions in the same places. Just as strong.'

'Did it wear off?'

'Yes—in a way. But it just comes back whenever I think about it.' He stopped. It felt as if he'd finished.

'Well, since you don't want my advice, I'll give it you. I'd say, stop going to the movies. I didn't know you liked them anyway.'

Graham didn't seem to be listening.

'You see, I told you about the *film* at such length because it was the catalyst. *That* was what sparked it all off. I mean, obviously I knew about some of Ann's chaps before me; I'd even met a few of them. Didn't know them all, of course. But it was only *after* the film that I started to care about them. It suddenly began to hurt that Ann had been to bed with them. It suddenly felt like ... I don't know — adultery, I suppose. Isn't that silly?'

'It's ... unexpected.' Jack deliberately didn't look up. Bonkers was the first word that had come to mind.

'It's silly. But I've begun thinking about them all in a different way. I've begun caring about them. I lie in bed waiting to go to sleep and it's like Richard the Third before that battle ... Whichever one it was.'

'Not your period?'

'Not my period. And half the time I'm wanting to line them all up in my head and take a good look at them, and half the time I'm too afraid to let myself do so. There are some whose names I know, but I don't know what they look like, and I just lie there filling in their faces, making up identikit pictures of them.'

'Hmmm. Anything else?'

'Well, I've tracked down a couple of other films Ann was in and gone to see them.'

'How much have you told Ann?'

'Not everything. Not about going to the films again. Just bits about getting upset.'

'And what does she say?'

'Oh, she says she's sorry I'm jealous, or possessive, or whatever the right word is, but it's quite unnecessary and it's nothing she's done — it isn't, of course — and maybe I'm overworking. I'm not.'

'Anything to be guilty about yourself? Any little naughties you might be transferring?'

'Christ no. If I was faithful to Barbara for fifteen years or whatever, I wouldn't be thinking of straying from Ann after this length of time.'

'Sure.'

'You don't say that very convincingly.'

'No, sure. In your case—*sure*.' He did sound convincing now.

'So what do I do?'

'I thought you didn't want advice?'

'No, I mean, where am I? Is any of this familiar to you?'

'Not really. I'm not too bad on current jealousies. I'm terrific on adultery—my type, not yours: I've got a good line of advice on *that* any time you need it. Well, all right ... But stuff in the past I'm not so hot on.' Jack paused. 'Of course, you could get Ann to lie to you. Get her to tell you she hadn't when she had.'

'No. Anyway, you can't do that. I'd never believe her when she told the truth.'

'Suppose not.' Jack thought he'd been very patient. He'd scarcely talked about himself for a long time. 'It's all a bit rarefied for me. Won't make a short story, I'm afraid.' It was odd how much people, even friends, imposed on you: just because you were a writer, they assumed you'd be interested in their problems.

'So you've no suggestions?'

And then—having told you they don't want advice, of course they do.

'Well, if it was me, I expect I'd go out and bang some tart for a cure.'

'Are you serious?'

'Perfectly.'

'How would that help?'

'You'd be surprised how that helps. Cures everything. Everything from a mild headache to writer's block. Very good for curing rows with the wife too.'

'We don't have rows.'

'Not at all? Well, I'll believe you. Sue and I row quite a bit. Always have—apart from the palmy days, of course. But then, we didn't bother to make the bed in the palmy

49

days; only rowed about who should go on top.' Graham's glasses had cleared; he could see Jack taking breath for anecdote. He should have remembered that Jack's attention, however protracted, was always conditional.

'With Valerie — don't think you ever met Val, did you? — I used to have rows all the time. Still, that was twenty years ago. But we used to have rows right from the start. Not your sort of milieu, old cunty; it was all *Room at the Top* and *A Kind of Loving* stuff. Hand up in the bus shelters. Trying to unsnap a suspender with two frozen fingers of your left hand when you're right-handed, while pretending you're really just stroking her thigh, *and* kissing her at the same time, *and* dropping your other mitt over her right shoulder and feeling for goodies. Makes it sound like bloody Clausewitz, doesn't it? Not too far wrong, either, now I come to think of it.

'So, first we'd have rows about where I put my hand when, how many fingers and so on. Then we finally had the Normandy landings, and I thought, well, okay, now the rows will stop. But they didn't; instead we had rows about how often, and when and where, and is that a fresh packet, Jack, will you *please* check the date on the side. Can you imagine — switching on the light in the middle to check the date on the packet?

'And after the Normandy landings, of course, we had the Battle of the Bulge. After we got married, of course. Then it was, should we, shouldn't we, why don't you get a proper job, look at this knitting pattern, and Margaret's had three already. Five or six years of that was enough, I can tell you. Buggered off down here.'

'What happened to Valerie?'

'Oh, Val, she married a teacher. Bit of a wet-panter, nice enough. Likes the kids, which is useful for me. Checks the date on the packet every time, I'm sure.'

Graham wasn't sure where Jack was leading, but he didn't mind too much. He'd never been let into Lupton history before: Jack's declared policy of living only in the present involved a stylized forgetting of the past. If asked about his early life, he would either refer you to his fiction, or invent a baroque lie on the spur of the moment. Of course, there was no knowing whether he wasn't even now trimming a myth to fit Graham's particular needs. Though always frank, the novelist was never wholly sincere.

'I thought I'd left the rows behind, up there with Val. When I met Sue, I thought, this is nice. No problem with the Normandy landings; well, there wouldn't have been—it was a dozen years later and *London*, and they'd built the bloody Channel tunnel by then, old matey, hadn't they? And Sue seemed less spiky than Val, at first. So we got married, and then, after a bit, guess what, the rows started. She'd begin by asking me what my role was, stuff like that. And I'd say, I'd like a role in bed with a little honey, please. And then we'd have a big row and I'd go off and have a bit of consolation, and then I'd come back and we'd have a row about *that*, so eventually I thought, well maybe it's me. Maybe I'm unlivable with. That was when we thought it would be better if I had the flat in town and she lived in the country. Well, you remember that—it was only a few years ago.'

'And?'

'And, guess what? We have just as many rows as before. Well, fewer in one sense, I suppose, because we see less of each other. But I'd say the number of rows per hour of contact with each other has remained completely stable. And we've got particularly good at having shouting matches on the phone. We have big rows about as often as when we lived together. And when we do, I take exactly the same course afterwards. I ring up an old girlfriend and get me some consolation. It always works. That's the thing I've discovered about what for want of a better word we may as well call adultery. It always works. If I were you, I'd go off and find myself a nice married woman.'

'Most of the women I've slept with *have* been married,'

51

said Graham. 'To me.' He felt depressed. He hadn't come to hear a version of Jack's life story; though he certainly hadn't minded hearing it. Nor had he come to learn about Jack's own private remedies. 'You're not seriously suggesting I go off and commit adultery?'

Jack laughed.

'Course I am. Second thoughts, course I'm not. You're much too much of a guilt-ridden granny for that. And you'd be bound to go straight home to Ann and blab it out on her shoulder, and *that* wouldn't do either of you any good or solve anything. No, all I'm saying is, that is your cross-eyed bear. Every marriage has a cross-eyed bear, and this is yours.'

Graham looked blankly at him.

'Cross-eyed bear. Cross You'd Bear? Cross I'd Bear? Okay? Fuckit, Graham, we've both been married twice, we're both practically clear of brain damage, we both thought about the whole thing each time before plunging into it. Now, four marriages tell us the honey time can't last. So what can you do about it? I mean, you don't think your present situation is Ann's *fault*, do you?'

'Of course not.'

'And you don't think it's yours?'

'No—I suppose I don't think about it in terms of fault.'

'Of course not. Quite right too. It's in the nature of the beast, that's what it is. It's in the nature of marriage. It's a design fault. There'll always be something, and the best way to survive, if you want to survive, is identify it, isolate it, and always make a particular response to it when it occurs.'

'Like you calling up an old girlfriend.'

'Sure. But you won't want to do that.'

'I can't think of anything relevant I might want to do. All I want to do is take a holiday from being inside my head.'

'Well, there are ways. Do something irrelevant if you like, but do it seriously. Have a wank, get drunk, go and buy a new tie. Doesn't matter what it is, just as long as you have some way of fighting back. Otherwise it'll get you down. Get you both down.'

Jack thought he was really doing quite well. He wasn't used to acting as a problem page, and he'd been fairly convinced by the plot structure he'd presented to Graham at such short notice. He'd managed to impose some sort of pattern on both their lives as he went along. Still, that was his job, after all, wasn't it: smelting order out of chaos, rendering fear and panic and agony and passion down into two hundred pages and six quid ninety-five. That was what he was paid to do, so this wasn't too hard a sideline. The percentage of lying was about the same as well.

Graham decided, though without much optimism, to think over what Jack had said. He'd always considered Jack more experienced than himself. Was he? They'd both been married twice, they'd both read about the same amount, they were of about the same intelligence. So why did he consider Jack an authority? Partly because Jack wrote books, and Graham respected books in both an abstract and a practical way, acknowledged a gut deference to their jurisdiction. And partly because Jack had had millions of affairs; always seemed to have a new girl in tow. Not that this necessarily made him an authority on marriage. But then, who was? Mickey Rooney? Zsa Zsa Gabor? Some Turkish sultan or other?

'Or ... ' said Jack. He was rubbing his beard and looking almost as serious as he could.

'Yes ... ?'

'Well, there's always one solution ... ' Graham sat up straighter in his chair. This was what he'd come for. Of *course*, Jack would know what to do, would know the right answer. That was why he'd come here; he knew he was right to come. ' ... You should love her less.'

'What?'

'Love her less. May sound a bit old-fashioned, but it'd work. You don't have to hate her or dislike her or anything

—don't go over the edge. Just learn to detach yourself a little. Be her friend if you like. Love her less.'

Graham hesitated. He didn't quite know where to begin. Eventually he said,

'I cry when the houseplants die.'

'Come again, squire?'

'She had these African violets. I mean, I don't like African violets much, and neither does Ann. I think she was given them. She's got lots of other plants she likes a lot more. And they got sort of plant chicken pox or something, and they died. Ann didn't mind at all. I went up to my study and cried. Not about *them*—I just found myself thinking about her watering them, and putting that fertilizer stuff on them, and, you know, not her feelings about the sodding plants— she didn't really have any, as I said—but her *time*, her *being there*, her *life* ...

'I'll tell you another thing. After she's gone to work, the first thing I do is take out my diary and write down everything she's got on. Shoes, tights, dress, bra, knickers, raincoat, hair-grip, rings. What colour. Everything. Often it's the same, of course, but I still write it down. And then occasionally, throughout the day, I take out my diary and look it up. I don't try and memorize what she's looking like—that'd be cheating. I get out my diary—sometimes when I'm teaching and pretend to be thinking about essay titles or something— and I sit there, sort of dressing her. It's very ... nice.

'I'll tell you another thing. I always clear the table after dinner. I go through to the kitchen, and I scrape my plate off into the kitchen bin, and then I suddenly find myself eating whatever she's left on hers. Often, you know, it isn't anything particularly nice—bits of fat and discoloured vegetables and sausage gristle—but I just scoff it. And then I go back and sit down opposite her, and I find myself thinking about our stomachs, about how whatever I've just eaten might easily have been inside her, but's inside me instead. I think, what an odd moment it must have been for that food, when the knife came down and the fork pushed it this way rather than that, and instead of lying inside you it's lying inside me. And that sort of makes me feel closer to Ann.

'And I'll tell you another thing. Sometimes, she gets up in the night and has a pee, and it's dark and she's half asleep and she somehow—God knows how she does it, but she does—she misses the bowl with the piece of paper she dries herself with. And I'll go in there in the morning and find it lying on the floor. And—it's not knicker-sniffing or anything like that—I sort of look at it and I feel ... soft. It's like one of those paper flowers that bad comedians wear in their buttonholes. It seems pretty, and colourful, and decorative. I could almost wear it in *my* buttonhole. I pick it up and shove it back in the bowl, but I feel sentimental afterwards.'

There was a silence. The two friends looked across at each other. Jack sensed a belligerence in Graham; the confession somehow managed to be aggressive. Perhaps too there was a touch of self-satisfaction about the recital. Jack felt almost embarrassed—so rare an occurrence that he began reflecting on his own internal condition rather than Graham's. Suddenly he became aware that his friend had stood up.

'Well, thanks, Jack.'

'Glad to be of any. If I was. Next time you need to give the old psychocouch a pounding just give me a buzz.'

'Yes I will. Thanks again.'

The front door was shut. Each had gone about five yards, in opposite directions, when they both paused. Jack paused while he gave a little pivot, a sort of fly-half's side-step in the middle of the hall. He farted, not very noisily, and commented to himself,

'Gone With the Wind.'

Outside, Graham paused, sniffed the dusty privet and the overflowing dustbins, and made a decision. If he cut out going to the good butcher, and did all his shopping at the supermarket, he could slip into *The Good Times* on his way home and catch Ann committing adultery again.

# FOUR

# *Sansepolcro, Poggibonsi*

And then it began to spread.

One evening in late March they were sitting over a map of Italy and discussing their holiday. Side by side on the bench at the kitchen table: Graham had an arm loosely dangled round Ann's shoulder. It was a comforting, marital arm, a tranquil parody of Jack's urgent, front-row forward's limb. Just looking at a map despatched Graham's mind on suave imaginings; he remembered how holidays made each old, familiar pleasure come up smelling like clean laundry. Vallombrosa, Camaldoli, Montevarchi, Sansepolcro, Poggibonsi, he read off to himself, and already he was in a cicada-crackling dusk, a glass of Chianti in his left hand, and his right hand floating up the inside of Ann's bare leg ... Bucine, Montepulciano, and he was being woken by the raucous flutter of a pheasant landing heavily outside their bedroom window to gorge with impunity on the bursting figs ... Then his eye tripped on

'Arezzo.'

'Yes, it's nice there. I haven't been for years.'

'No. Yes, I mean, I know. Arezzo.' Suddenly Graham's lolling fantasies were over.

'You haven't been, have you, love?' Ann asked him.

'Don't know. Don't remember. Doesn't matter.' He stared back at the map, but it blurred as a tear eased itself into his left eye. 'No, I was just remembering that you once told me you went to Arezzo with Benny.'

'Did I? So I did. God, that feels years ago. It was, too. It must have been ten years at least. Probably in the Sixties. Think of that: *in the Sixties*.' She was briefly jarred by pleasure at the thought that she had been doing interesting, grown-up things for such a length of time; for at least fifteen years, and she was still only thirty-five. A fuller, happier person now; and one still young enough not to flag at pleasure. She pressed closer to Graham on the bench.

'You went to Arezzo with Benny,' he repeated.

'Yes. Do you know, I can't remember anything about it. Is that where that great, sort of bowl-shaped square is? Or is that Siena?'

'That's Siena.'

'Then Arezzo ... that must be the place where ... ' She frowned, in disapproval of her bad memory as much as in an attempt to search it. 'I can only remember going to the cinema in Arezzo.'

'You went to the cinema in Arezzo,' said Graham slowly, in the tone of one prompting a child, 'and you saw a bad sentimental comedy about a whore who tries to disgrace the village priest, and then you came out and sat over an iced Strega in the only café you could find that was open, and you wondered as you drank how you could ever again live in a climate that was damp and cold, and then you went back to your hotel and you ... screwed Benny as if you would never know greater pleasure, and you held nothing back from him, absolutely nothing, you didn't even save a small corner of your heart and leave it untouched for when you met me.'

It was all uttered in a sad, hurt way, almost too precise to be self-indulgent. Was he putting it on? Was any of it a joke? As Ann looked across to check up, he went on,

'I made up the last part of course.'

'Of course. I never said anything like that to you, did I?'

'No, you told me as far as the café, and I guessed the other things. Something about your expression told me the rest.'

'Well, I don't know if it's true; I don't remember. And anyway, Graham, I was twenty, twenty-one, I'd never been to Italy before. I'd never been on holiday with anyone who was as nice to me as Benny.'

'Or had as much money.'

'Or had as much money. Is that wrong?'

'No. I can't explain it. I certainly can't justify it. I'm glad you went to Italy. I'm glad you didn't go alone; it might have been dangerous. I'm glad you went with someone who was nice to you. I'm glad—I suppose I have to be—that you went to bed with him there. I know it all in steps, I know the logic. All of it makes me glad. It just makes me want to cry as well.'

Ann said gently,

'I didn't know you then.' She kissed him on the temple, and stroked the far side of his head, as if to calm the sudden turbulence inside. 'And if I *had* known you then, I'd have wanted to go with you. But I didn't know you. So I couldn't. It's as simple as that.'

'Yes.' It was simple. He gazed at the map, following the route he knew Ann had taken with Benny a decade before he had met her. Down the coast, through Genoa to Pisa, across to Florence, Rimini, Urbino, Perugia, Arezzo, Siena, back to Pisa and up again. Benny had just removed a great slice out of Italy for him. He might as well take a pair of scissors to the map, shear straight across it from Pisa to Rimini, cut a parallel line through Assisi, and then stick the bottom bit of Italy back on to what was now left of the top bit. Make it into a mere bootee—the sort with little buttons down the side. As worn by posh whores; or so he imagined.

They could go to Ravenna, he supposed. He hated mosaics. He really hated mosaics. Benny had left him with the mosaics. Thanks very much, Benny.

'We could go to Bologna,' he said finally.

'You've been to Bologna before.'

'Yes.'

'You went to Bologna with Barbara.'

'Yes.'

'You almost certainly slept in the same bed as Barbara in Bologna.'

'Yes.'

'Well, Bologna's fine with me. Is it a nice place to go?'

'I've forgotten.'

Graham stared at the map again. Ann stroked the side of his head, trying not to feel guilty about what she knew it would be foolish to begin feeling guilty about. After a few minutes' contemplation Graham said quietly,

'Ann ... '

'Yes?'

'When you went to Italy ... '

'Yes?'

'With Benny ... '

'Yes?'

'Was there ... was there ... I was just wondering ... '

'It's better to say it than not to say it.'

'Was there ... well, was there ... I shouldn't think you can remember ... ' He looked at her mournfully, pleadingly, hopefully. She longed to be able to give him the answer he wanted. ' ... But was there anywhere you went that you can remember—that you can remember *definitely* ... '

'Yes, love?'

' ... that you had the curse?'

They began to laugh quietly together. They kissed a little awkwardly, as if neither of them had expected to kiss; and then Ann firmly folded up the map.

But the next day, when Graham got home a few hours before Ann, he found himself straying back to her book-shelves. He knelt in front of the third shelf from the bottom and looked at her travel books. A couple of guides to London, one to the Pennines—they didn't mean anything. A student guide to San Francisco; James Morris on Venice; Companion Guides to Florence (of course) and the South of

France; Germany, Spain, Los Angeles, India. He didn't know she'd been to India. Who'd she been to India with, he wondered; though with not much zest, or jealousy for that matter, perhaps because he had little desire to go there himself.

He pulled out the handful of maps wedged at the end of the shelf. It was hard to tell straightaway which cities they were of, because Ann hadn't bothered to fold them back—as he would have done—so that the title page was on the outside. He wondered if this carelessness was common to most women; he wouldn't be surprised if it were. Women, after all, were unreliable in their spatial and geographical awareness. They often had no natural sense of North; some even had problems telling left from right (like Alison, his first girlfriend; whenever she was asked to give directions in a car, she would hold up a fist and look at it—as if there were a big sticky label on its back saying either RIGHT or LEFT—and then read off to the driver what her hand said). Was it all conditioning, he wondered; or brain structure?

Women, it seemed, also had no easily acquired mental map of cities. Graham had once seen an illustration of the human body in which the size of each part was represented according to the sensitivity of its surface area: the resulting homunculus displayed an enormous head with African lips, hands like baseball gloves, and a thin, pickled body in between. He ought to have remembered the size of the genitals, but couldn't. Ann's private map of London, he thought, would be similarly distorted and unbalanced: at its southern end a vastly inflated Clapham, leading by a series of wide arteries to Soho, Bloomsbury, Islington and Hampstead; there would be an inflated bubble down towards Knightsbridge, and another across at Kew; while joining them up would be lots of jumbled areas with names in tiny print: Hornsey on top of Ealing and south of Stepney, the Isle of Dogs moored next to Chiswick Eyot.

Perhaps this was why women—Graham now made the

smooth generalization out from Ann—never folded maps up properly: because the overall conception of the city was unimportant to them, so that there was no 'right order' from which to start. All of Ann's maps had been put away as if they'd been interrupted in mid-use. This made them more personal and, Graham suddenly realized, more threatening to him. A map, for him, once folded back into its proper order, lost its user's stamp: it could be lent or given away without touching on any feelings of attachment. Looking at Ann's awkwardly squashed maps with their overruled creases was like seeing a clock stopped at a certain, significant time; or—and worse, he realized—like reading her diary. Some of the maps (Paris, Salzburg, Madrid) had biro marks on them: crosses, circles, street numbers. The sudden particularities of a life previous to him. He stuffed the maps back into their place.

Later that evening he asked, in as mild and neutral a tone as he could manage,

'Ever fancy going to India?'

'Oh, we wouldn't want to go there, would we?' Ann seemed quite surprised.

'I don't much; I just wondered if you'd ever been interested.'

'I think I was once, and I read up about it, but it seemed depressing, so I gave up wanting to go.'

Graham nodded. Ann looked quizzically at him; but he didn't answer her unspoken why, and she decided not to voice it.

After that he stopped worrying about India. He worried a lot about Italy, and Los Angeles, and the South of France, and Spain and Germany, but he did at least have no cause to worry about India. There was not a single Indian in India, he reflected, who had ever seen Ann walking side by side with someone who wasn't him. That was a solid, unshiftable fact. It left, of course, all the Indians in England, Italy, Los Angeles, the South of France, Spain and Germany, any number of whom might have seen her arm in arm with Benny or Chris or Lyman or Phil or whoever. But these Indians were vastly outweighed by Indian Indians, absolutely none of whom (except perhaps on an overseas holiday —now that was a thought) could ever possibly have so seen her.

India was safe. South America was safe. Japan and China were safe. Africa was safe. Europe and North America weren't safe. When the television news came on with stories about Europe or the States, he occasionally found his attention wandering. When he read the morning paper he often skimmed the unsafe areas of the world; but since he still allowed the same amount of time for the paper as before, he gradually found himself knowing a lot more about India and Africa than he ever needed, or indeed wanted, to know. Quite without any serious inquisitiveness he managed to acquire a thorough familiarity with Indian politics. He knew about Japan too. In the departmental common room he found himself turning to Bailey, a scruffy gerontologist who had wandered in by mistake, and saying,

'Did you see that Narita airport lost sixteen million pounds in its first four months of operation?' To which Bailey had replied interestedly,

'Male menopause already?'

On his afternoons alone at the house, Graham found himself more and more on the lookout for evidence. Sometimes he wasn't sure what constituted evidence; and sometimes, in the course of his forays, he wondered whether he didn't secretly enjoy finding that proof which he told himself he feared and hated. The effect of his driven searches was to re-acquaint himself with almost all of Ann's possessions; only now he saw them in a different, more tainted light.

He opened the walnut box in which she kept her foreign coins. Inside, it was divided into twelve square sections, each compartment lined with purple velvet. Graham stared at the leftover currency. Lire meant Benny, or that other fellow, or

—well, he had to admit it—himself, and their five days in Venice after they were married. Nickels, quarters and a single silver dollar meant Lyman. Francs meant Phil, or that creep with the jeep—Jed, or whatever he called himself. Marks meant, oh stuff it. And this, Graham thought, picking up a large silver coin, what about this? He read round its edge: R.IMP.HU.BO.REG.M.THERESIA.D.G. Then the other side: ARCHID.AUSTR.DUX.BURG.CO.TY.1780.X. He smiled to himself. A Maria Theresa krone. Nothing doing *there*, at least.

He played the same game with her wicker basket full of book matches. She didn't smoke, but collected matches from restaurants, hotels, clubs—anywhere that gave them away. The only difficulty he struck, as he rooted through the relics of careless cocktails and drunken dinners, of dozens upon dozens of wholly Grahamless occasions, was working out whether or not Ann had actually been to the places whose free publicity he was now sifting. Friends knew her collecting habit, and would look out for particularly garish or obscure items to add to her basket. Graham had even encouraged them to. So how could he get his bearings? There was no point in getting jealous unless you were accurate about it; or so it seemed to Graham.

Irritated by this uncertainty, he moved on to Ann's shelves and started hunting for books which she was unlikely to have bought for herself. Several of them he had already identified as presents from her previous escorts. These he pulled out, almost for old times' sake, and read the inscriptions: 'to my ... ', 'with love from', 'with much love from', 'love and kisses from', 'x x x from'. What a dreary bunch, Graham thought: they might as well get some printed labels if that's all they were going to say. Then he pulled out Ann's copy of *Gormenghast*. 'To my little squirrel, who always remembers where the nuts are kept'. Bloody Jed—yes he was called Jed, as the scrawny signature of a quite well-educated orang-utan confirmed; the creep with the jeep. Yes, well, that was expected. He would have given her *Gormenghast*. At least the bookmark showed she hadn't got past page thirty. Quite right too. *Gormenghast*, he repeated contemptuously to himself. And *Jed*. What had Ann once said about him? 'It was a brief, therapeutic affair.' Therapeutic? Well, he supposed he could understand. And brief: he was pleased about that, and not just for the obvious reason. He didn't want the house cluttered up with the collected works of Tolkien and Richard Adams as well.

Graham began to play a game with himself, based on Strip Jack Naked. He had to find the books on Ann's shelves which had been given her by other people. If he didn't find one such book in four tries, he lost the game. If he got one on the fourth go, he had another turn; if he got one after only two gos, he saved himself two gos, and so had six chances in the next round.

With just a little cheating he managed to keep this game going for about twenty minutes, though by that time the pleasure of the hunt obscured less and less adequately the glumness of victory. As he sat on the floor and looked at the pile of books which represented his winnings, he felt the approach of a daunting sadness. On top lay a copy of *The End of the Affair*. 'Don't think unkindly of me. It has been wonderful. In time you'll see that too. It's been almost too good. M.' Ha—Michael. Just the sort of prickish thing he would put. *It's been almost too good*. What he really meant was, 'Why didn't you behave badly so that I could leave you without any guilt?' Michael, the good-looking sporty one with—so Ann assured him—an engaging way of shaking his head and blinking shyly at you. That was how Ann had described him. Graham thought of him as the prick with the tic.

It made him sad. It made him feel aggressive in an unfocused way, and it made him feel self-pitying; but mostly it made him feel straight sad. Perhaps now was the right time to try one of Jack's solutions. Not that he'd gone to Jack for solutions; not really. But it was a harmless thing to try. Well, he thought harmless. And Ann wouldn't be home for at least an hour and a half.

Graham went to his study with a certain feeling of self-mockery. Apart from anything else, it was silly that his study was the only safe hiding-place. He pulled out a drawer of his filing cabinet; the drawer marked 1915–19. The manila files all presented their open sides to the eye, except for one. This he took out, turned the right way up, and extracted from it a pink, candy-striped paper-bag. Where to go? Not downstairs, in case Ann came back unexpectedly. Not in the bedroom — that would be far too much like adultery. Stay here? But where? Not at his desk; that would feel all wrong. He decided reluctantly on the bathroom.

Graham hadn't masturbated since he was eighteen, since the evening before the morning when he'd asked Alison, his first girlfriend, for a date. That decision had increased his confidence about asking her out, and so afterwards, in pious gratitude, he'd made his renunciation final. Besides, he hadn't been happy about the guilt. He'd always masturbated in the lavatory at home; either before or immediately after his colonic activities, so that if he was quizzed about where he'd been, he wouldn't actually be lying. This reduced the guilt a little, but it still hung around sycophantically.

He also hadn't masturbated, he realized, since the days when people thought about it as 'masturbation': that cool, frowning medico-Biblical word. There'd been other words around, no doubt, but 'masturbation' was what it always felt like. Masturbation, fornication, defecation: serious words from his childhood, representing activities to be pondered before being indulged in. Nowadays it was all wanking and fucking and shitting, and no one thought twice about any of them. Well, he used shitting himself; a bit, privately. Jack, of course, talked about wanking quite casually, and fucking as well. Graham was still a little tentative about both usages. 'Wanking', after all, was such a quiet, domestic, guiltless sort of word: it made it sound like a home craft.

Twenty-two years since he had last masturbated. Wanked. And several different flats and houses where he hadn't. He sat on the lavatory seat and looked around; then got up and pulled the cork-topped linen box over towards him. Where it had come from there were four sharp depressions in the carpet, one at each corner of a rectangle of dust. Graham settled back on the lavatory seat, pulled the linen box in closer and put his paper bag on top of it. Then he lowered his trousers and pants to his ankles.

That didn't feel very comfortable. He stood up, closed the lid of the lavatory, and laid a towel across the top. Then he settled back. He took a breath, reached into the bag and pulled out the two magazines he had hastily bought from an Indian newsagent on his way back from a distant cinema. He'd tried to look puzzled when he bought them, as if they were really for someone else; but he expected he had only managed to look furtive.

One was *Penthouse*, which he'd heard of; the other *Rapier*, which he hadn't. He laid them side by side on the linen box and read the contents lists on the covers. He wondered about the title of *Rapier*. Was it meant to indicate a world of buccaneering sexuality, where Errol Flynn was king? Or was it merely, perhaps, the comparative form of the adjective 'rapy'? Rapier than thou?

The two girls on the covers, each, by some magazine publishers' convention, exposing only one nipple, struck Graham as extremely beautiful. Why did such girls need to take their clothes off? Or was there some connection between being extremely beautiful and *wanting* to take your clothes off? Most likely, the connection was between being extremely beautiful and being offered helpful sums of money to take your clothes off. He expected that was it.

He took a deep breath, looked down at what he used to call his penis but now wasn't so sure, grasped it in his right hand, and turned the cover of *Rapier* with his left. Another contents page, illustrated this time by a photograph of a

66

deep, pink ravine, topped with a tropical rain forest. It had been raining in the ravine too, by the look of it. Graham was fascinated and slightly appalled. Next came a few pages of readers' letters, also illustrated with topographical shots, then an eight-page photo-spread of another extremely beautiful girl. On the first page she was sitting in a wicker chair wearing only a pair of knickers; then she was naked and playing with her nipple; then with her ... down there anyway; until by the eighth page she appeared to be trying to turn her ... thing inside out, as if it were a trouser pocket. On this last page, while Graham's brain gawped, his semen (as he used to think of it, but now also wasn't quite sure) came spurting out, quite unexpectedly. It sprayed over the left arm of his sweater, over the linen box, and over the girl contortionist.

In a panic, as if he had a maximum of two seconds in which to do it, Graham seized some lavatory paper and began swabbing down his sleeve, his magazine, his for want of a better word penis, and the linen box. To his dismay he saw that the cork top of the box now bore several damp, rather slimy marks. He flushed the soggy paper down the lavatory and wondered what to do. The stains somehow didn't look like simple water stains. What could he say he'd spilt — aftershave? shampoo? He thought of dribbling a few drops of shampoo on to the linen box as well, so that when Ann asked (as when his father had asked) he could at least not lie to her. But what if the shampoo made a different sort of mark? Then he'd have to say he'd spilt some shampoo *and* some aftershave. That didn't sound very likely. Then he realized he'd been in the bathroom for barely five minutes. Ann still wouldn't be back for ages. He could sit it out and see what happened to the stains.

It hadn't been a particularly good ... wank, as he supposed he'd better start calling it. Too short, too sudden, and too alarming at the end to be consciously enjoyed. But then he'd been more than surprised by his material. He leaned back against the lavatory cistern and opened *Penthouse*. He read the list of contents and turned to the drink column. Sound enough; if rather jocosely written. Then the motoring column, a fashion feature, and a science fiction story about what would happen to men when robots could be built which were not only better lovers than their fleshly rivals, but were also capable of impregnating women. Then he read the letters column, and the editorial replies, which struck him as full of sound advice.

By this time he noticed two occurrences: his cock, as he now thought he would call it, was beginning to get hard again while he read a letter from a Surrey housewife gratified by the number of dildoid-shaped objects available to the dedicated self-pleasurer; and his semen (he didn't feel ready for spunk yet) seemed to have quite dried out. In for a penny, he said to himself jollily, and began to wank again, only this time with more care, interest and pleasure, at the beginning, and in the middle, and at the end.

# FIVE

# Sawn-Offs and Four-Eyes

'Well, well, well, my little birdy. Now this is what the poet calls a surprise.'

'Jack, are you busy? I won't stay long.'

'Well, it's not the greatest come-on I've heard, but it'll do.'

Jack squashed himself none too efficiently against the wall, and felt Ann brush him slightly as she went past. She walked quickly into his long, all-purpose room and sat down without hesitation. Jack closed the front door carefully and followed her, smiling a little.

'Coffee?' Ann declined with her head. She was looking as pretty nowadays as Jack could ever remember: a smart, serious prettiness, all of whose elements matched.

'Jack, I've come to get history straight.'

'Oh dear. I thought it was going to be another session of marriage guidance. And I don't mind telling you which partner I'd rather see stretched out on my couch.'

'You were very kind to Graham.'

'Didn't do much. Just made up some stuff, as far as I can remember, along the lines of buying himself a new hat when he felt glum. Nearly told him all men really have the curse, but I didn't think he'd swallow it.'

'Well, he seemed calmer when he got home. He seemed to appreciate it.'

'Any time.'

Jack was standing in front of her, brown and squat, rocking backwards on his heels. He always looked a bit Welsh, she thought, though he wasn't. He was wearing a brown tweed suit, an old leather waistcoat and a workman's shirt; the gold stud threaded through the collar band was strictly for decoration. Ann had often wondered about the way Jack presented himself to the world: was he dressing down, in pursuit of a remembered or imagined yeoman simplicity; or was he dressing up, in pursuit of artistic carelessness? She had always been fobbed off when she'd asked serious quessions about Jack's past; but didn't mind. This time, however, she'd come to discuss her own past.

'Jack,' she said slowly, 'I've decided we never had an affair.'

He was going to laugh, but noticed how serious she was looking. Instead, he took his hands out of his pockets, brought his heels together and said sharply,

'*Sah*!'

'It came up last night. We were ... well, Graham was listing some of my old boyfriends to me. He was a bit drunk. We were both a bit drunk. We seem to get drunk more often nowadays. Then he started crying, drinking and crying. I asked him what the matter was and he said the name of one of my old boyfriends. He just said "Benny". Then he took another swig of wine and said, "Benny and Jed". Then he took another swig and said, "Benny and Jed and Michael". It was awful.'

'Doesn't sound much fun.'

'And each time he took a swig he'd say the names, and each time he said the names he'd add a new one. And then he'd cry a bit more and take another swig.' Ann reached for a tissue at the memory. 'And then, after he'd been going for a while he suddenly added your name.'

'And that was a surprise?'

'Completely. At first I thought you must have told him about us when he came to see you, but then I thought that if you had, he wouldn't have come home so cheerful. So I just said, "No, Graham", quite firmly.'

'Dead right, too.'

'I felt a bit bad, because I don't think I've lied to him before. I mean, the usual stuff about the tubes being held up or whatever, but nothing ... like that.'

'Well, you know my rule about affairs: maximum deception, minimum lying, maximum kindness. Don't see why it shouldn't apply to ones in the past as well.'

'So I'm afraid I said No. I was sure you'd understand.'

'Of course.' In fact, Jack was a bit hurt; it felt as it did when someone turned you down, which was silly, though in a way accurate. 'No problem. Pity about that chapter of the old autobiography, though. Would have bumped up the advance.'

'I'm sorry to rewrite your past for you.'

'Don't bother, I'm always doing it myself. Every time I tell a story it's different. Can't remember how most of them started off any more. Don't know what's true. Don't know where I came from.' He put on a sad look, as if someone had stolen his childhood. 'Ah well, just part of the pain and pleasure of the artist's life.' He was beginning to fictionalize his fictioneering already; Ann smiled. 'But what about friends?'

'Well, it hasn't ever arisen so far, and a lot of those friends are in the past.'

'Hm. This may sound a trifle ungallant, but can you remind me when it was that we didn't have an affair? '74? '73?'

'Autumn of '72 to summer of '73. And ... and once or twice subsequently.'

'Ah yes. I remember once or twice.' He smiled. Ann smiled back, but with less confidence.

'I might tell Graham sometime — when he's ... over ... this. I mean, if it's relevant, or if he asks or something.'

'And then my past will be restored to me. O frabjous day, calloo, callay. And what is the current prognosis? How is the little Othello?'

Ann was hurt by Jack's frivolity of tone.

71

'He's having a bad time. It may seem ludicrous to you, and it sometimes seems it to me, but he's having a bad time. I sometimes worry he doesn't seem to think about anything else. At least he's got his work.'

'Yes, that's a good thing.'

'Except that the vacation's coming up.'

'Well, keep him occupied. Take him off somewhere.'

'We're trying to find some country where I haven't fucked someone,' Ann said with sudden bitterness.

Jack kept any further thoughts to himself. He'd always been fond of Ann, even when, in what he now knew to be the summer of 1973, they'd fallen out over some self-indulgent indiscretion of his, some bit of double-parking. He always thought of her as a no-shit girl; maybe not sparky enough for his taste, but definitely a no-shit girl. As he showed her out, he pushed his face at her for a kiss. She moved towards him, hesitated, and scraped her cheek along the side of his beard; as she moved away, Jack's slightly wetted lips seemed to catch her ear.

Barbara was sitting on the sofa in her nylon housecoat, sipping at a cup of tea and brooding idly about Graham. She thought about him a little more often than in her view he deserved. The initial contempt had died down by now, and even resentment, that normally reliable emotion, no longer invaded her as it had for the first couple of years. This didn't mean, of course, that she had in any way forgiven Graham, or liked him, or even 'saw his point of view'—that thing which her feebler or more disloyal friends occasionally urged her to do. The same friends also suggested, in their bolder moments, that in some way she was just unlucky, that a certain percentage of marriages always went wrong, that it was nobody's fault, that it was the way of the world. To them she would reply,

'I'm still here. Alice is still here. The *house* is still here. Even the car is still here. All that has happened is that

Graham has run off.' This uncoloured recital of fact usually sent enquirers off in the wrong direction:

'So you ... well, you might have him back if ... if ... '

'Of course not. Out of the question.' And she meant it.

When she thought of Graham nowadays she saw two pictures of him. The first was of him rearing above her while they were making love on the night of their eighth wedding anniversary. On these nights, she always allowed Graham to keep the light on. He was crouched over her, pushing away in that rather half-hearted fashion which at any rate seemed to satisfy him, when she had caught him looking at her breasts. That was all right in itself, of course: it was —partly —why she allowed him to keep the light on in the first place. But it was the way he was looking at them. It wasn't distaste, exactly, nor was it lack of interest that she saw in his face. It was more insulting than that: there was a scintilla of interest present, vaguely benign but humiliatingly small. She had seen that look before. It was the expression of a supermarket shopper who doesn't need anything from the deep freeze but still peers briefly and ritually into it.

After that, on their wedding anniversaries, Barbara decreed that either they could have the light on and read a bit, or they could turn it off and make love. It was all the same to her, she implied. More frequently, in latter years, they had kept the light on.

Her other picture of Graham was also of him kneeling — this time half-askew on the stairs. How many years ago? She couldn't remember. His left knee was on a higher step than his right knee; his bottom was sticking out. He was a third of the way up, yellow plastic brush in the right hand, matching pan in the left. He finished one step and moved on to the one above it. He was helping her out because he was on holiday and she was feeling tired. She looked up at his protruding bottom, at the yellow brush dabbing fussily at the carpet, and passed on through into the sitting-room. A couple of minutes later she returned to the hall. He had one stair left to do. When he reached the top, he turned, a school-boy expecting a gold paper star to be stuck at the foot of his homework.

'If you start at the top,' she had merely said, 'and work downwards, then all the dust gets brushed down.' For God's sake, he was a teacher, an academic, I mean, he was meant to be bright, wasn't he?

And half-askew as he was, looking back over his shoulder, he gave her another schoolboy look. It's not my fault I cacked my pants, *it's not my fault*. Don't blame me. He looked (she had sought the playground word to fit) so *weedy*. Bill and Ben, Flowerpot Men, she thought; and in between them, as they clunked woodenly about on their strings, had been Little Weed. 'Hallo, Weeeeeeeeeed,' her friends used to say to one another at school. She had almost said it then.

Meanwhile, at home, Graham was taking a chicken out of the refrigerator. He slipped the bird from its polythene wrapping and placed it on the chopping board. Then he picked it up by the wings and shook it vigorously. The bag of giblets fell from the broad hole between the chicken's legs, and Graham muttered,

'It's a boy.'

He pushed the bag aside and began jointing the chicken, with vigour rather than sense. He wrenched off the wings, then wound the legs round like propellors until, with a sudden crack, they gave way. He stared briefly at the skin on one of the legs. Bumpy and puckered: like the skin of his scrotum.

Graham took a cleaver from the magnetic rack above his head, and brought it down sharply on the chicken's breast-bone. He did this two or three more times until the carcase gave way. He chopped some more; the occasional bone splintered, and he tried half-heartedly to pick out the loose shards.

He tossed the ragged chunks of meat into a frying pan for

browning. Then he picked up the cleaver again and moved the plastic bag of giblets back into the centre of the board. He stared at it for about a minute, then chopped down very hard several times, in quick succession, as if he had to get the blows in before the giblets panicked and ran off. As the bag split, blood jumped at his wrist, at the board, and at the blue-striped plastic apron that he wore. He dragged the entrails together again with the back of the cleaver and gave them several more swift cuts. He enjoyed this, in an uncomplicated way. He smiled. They said work was the best cure for sadness; but this was just as good.

Graham smiled again. He wondered if they made Jiffy bags with plastic linings.

Naturally, Ann didn't tell Graham about her visit to Repton Gardens. When, the next afternoon, Jack opened his door and found Graham whispering fiercely,

'I'm not really here — you won't tell Ann, will you?'
he couldn't resist a grin. First they start rewriting the past; now they're rewriting the present as it happens. If only they could control the future they'd be able to have it all their own way.

'Course not, matey.'

'You're not working?'

'No. Just gussying up a review. Come along in.'

They went into Jack's chaotic sitting-room. Graham sat in the same chair as before; Jack made him coffee in the same mug as before, and then waited. Graham seemed keen to reproduce the same initial pause as well. Jack was less patient this time.

'Did you take the tablets?'

'Sort of. I mean you said three things. I've been doing about one and a half of them. I didn't go and buy any new clothes; I didn't think that would work.' (Christ, Jack reflected, he *had* taken him seriously; not exactly a figure-of-speech merchant, our Graham). 'And I suppose I was

75

drinking a bit anyway, so I just carried on doing that, which counts as the half.'

Jack couldn't remember what else he'd suggested; all he could recall was talking rather too openly about his first marriage.

'And I've mas ... I've mas ... wanked.' Graham looked so academic as he spoke the words.

'You've mass-wanked? Good on you. Who are the lucky guys?'

Graham smiled wanly. Jack marvelled at how seriously people seemed to take sex; how much, how extraordinarily much it had them by the balls.

'It's not the end of the world, old cunty. I mean, I didn't notice the whole shooting-match shift on its axis at whatever time it was you did it.'

'I hadn't done it for twenty years.'

'Cheeeerist. Really? What was it like? Tell me. Please tell me. I always remember only too well.'

'It was ... ' Graham paused; Jack began a pre-emptive wince, ' ... enjoyable.' Jack exhaled with relief in a vigorous, short mouth-plop.

'Too right. So why the straight face?'

'Oh, well, couple of things really. You see, I bought a magazine to do it with.'

'So? Most of us have a library under our beds. Want to borrow some?'

'Er, no thanks.'

'Any time.'

'And you see, I enjoyed it and I used a magazine, and I didn't feel guilty towards Ann.'

'And you've done it again?' Jack felt like a zealous priest, prompting Graham towards total admission of his in this case sinless deeds.

'Oh, yes, several times as a matter of fact.'

'So you've found your touch again, eh? None of that shooting off over a double-page spread of a Nikon camera?'

Graham grinned in acknowledgment of one of his early difficulties.

'But do you think I *should* feel guilty towards Ann?'

'Nope.'

'Do you think I should tell her?'

'You haven't?'

'No.'

'Well, I'd leave it until she asks. I mean, we all do it—read your Kinsey. Ninety-eight per cent have at some time, and 96 per cent are still doing so. Something like that, you know figures aren't my strong point. But, well, only 2 per cent stop on marriage. It's a fact, Graham.'

Jack wasn't completely sure that it was a fact; but it was good enough for Graham's purposes.

'Do you think—I mean, do you think it will interfere with, with the rest of it all?'

Sometimes Graham's questions weren't phrased as clearly as they might be; Jack hoped his friend didn't set examination papers as imprecisely as this.

'No, absolutely not. Doesn't affect it at all. Keeps it smoothly oiled.'

'Can ... ' Graham halted again. 'Can ... *they* ... ' (Graham didn't like using Jack's collective pronoun; but couldn't bear to specify Ann) ' ... tell? I mean, whether you've been doing it?'

'No way. No way. Not unless they've got a measuring glass up there or something. You know—calibrated cunt. I don't think it registers cubic millimetres that finely.'

'Ah.' Graham set down his coffee mug. 'The other thing,' he looked across at Jack in an accusing manner, 'is that it doesn't work.'

'Eh? You just said it did. Didn't you?'

'No. *It* works; *it* works fine' (he supposed 'it' did) 'but doing...*it* hasn't had any effect on the rest. I've seen *The G*...one of those films I go to three times this week. I've seen another one as well. I buy all those papers which tell you what's on.'

'Look, I didn't say wanking would stop you going to the movies, did I?'

'I thought you did.'

'No, all I said was that *at best* it might be a consolation if you got cut up about … stuff. I can't tell you anything to stop you wanting to go to the movies. I mean, that's in your head, isn't it?'

'Can't you do anything about my head?' The appeal was almost pathetic.

'Heads,' Jack pronounced definitively, 'is heads.' He rummaged down into his chair and lit a cigarette. 'Been reading this tome of Koestler's. Well, started it, anyway.' (Jack could speak with authority about books glimpsed over a stranger's shoulder in a crowded tube train.) 'He says, or at any rate he says other boffins say, that the old brainbox isn't at all like we imagine. We all believe it's a big deal, our brain. We all think it's the shit-hot part of us — I mean, it stands to reason, doesn't it, that's why we aren't monkeys or foreigners. Computer technology, latest I.B.M. equipment in there. Not so?'

Graham nodded. That's what he'd always believed, if ever he'd thought about it.

'Not so. No way. The boffin cunts, apparently, or some of them anyway, say *bits* of it are like that. Trouble is, there are a couple of other layers, different colours or something, don't quote me. *One* lot of these little cell buggers have been developing away like hell all these years, working on fuel-injection and zips and publishers' contracts and stuff. They're all right; they're quite socially acceptable. But the *other* lot, even though they've been busting a gut for millennia trying to improve themselves — you know, fucking each other the way cells do, press-ups every morning, working out on Muscle Beach — they're found it's no dice. Strictly no dice. They've got the wrong genes, or whatever cells have. They've reached their peak level, and they've got to face up to the fact that they're really pretty dim. That's O.K. for them—I mean, they don't have anywhere to go, do they? They don't go dancing on a Saturday night, do they? They're just there to fuck us up or not fuck us up as the case may be.'

Jack paused. He liked pauses like this in his stories. It made him feel he was not only a novelist, but—that phrase he read often but still all too rarely in his cuttings—a born storyteller. One reviewer had once written of him: 'With Lupton, you can trust the teller *and* the tale.' He'd sent him a case of champagne.

'And as the case is, they *do* fuck us up. Because that lot, the second eleven, they're the ones that control our emotions, make us kill people, fuck other people's wives, vote Tory, kick the dog.'

Graham looked at him carefully.

'So it's not our fault?'

'Ah. Didn't say that, old chap. Won't be drawn on that one. I'll write you a book on the subject, but if you want me to talk about it—well, you wouldn't be able to afford the fee for a start. That's campus stuff and foreign exchange.'

'So?'

'So?'

'So—do you think there's any truth in it?'

'Ah. Well. I don't know. Shouldn't think so. I mean, I just thought it was an interesting theory. Thought it might make you feel better. Make you think of your skull in a different way: one layer of Four-Eyes, two layers of Sawn-Offs. Now why don't they get together, you ask; why don't they sit down at the conference table with some cerebral U Thant and just thrash out their difficulties? Why do the Sawn-Offs keep fucking up the achievements of the Four-Eyes? Eh? I mean, you'd think the Sawn-Offs would *see* it was in their interests to keep their tiny heads down, not rock the boat ... '

'What do you think?' Graham genuinely wanted to know.

'Ah.' Jack, while elaborating his United Nations line, had kept a small part of his brain working on that one. What would be the best answer? What would Graham want to hear? 'Well. My considered is, probably no; that's my considered.'

He got up, walked around pretending to be looking for a cigarette, returned, did a peg-leg swivel, farted, and murmured, as he 'found' his cigarettes on the arm of his chair, 'The Wind and Wisdom of Jack Lupton.'

He grinned; he'd extracted that from another, even smaller compartment of his mind; probably one occupied by Sawn-Offs, but then you never needed full power for puns. 'My considered says, might be true for a few — I mean, don't they think criminals have a defective gene; something gives a little pop in their skull and suddenly they're under the stairs again digging out the striped sweater and the sack marked SWAG. Maybe for crims. But most people? Most people don't kill other people. Most people have got the Sawn-Offs well under their thumb, I'd say. Most people control their emotions, don't they? It may not be easy, but they do. I mean, they control them *enough*, don't they, and that's what it's all about, that's what we're talking about. And without embarking on the neurology of it, I'd say that either the second eleven know which side their bread's buttered, or perhaps the prefects really know how to handle them.'

'But you fuck, as you put it, other people's wives.'

'Eh? What's that got to do with it?'

'Well, you said that's one of the things the underdeveloped part of your brain made you do. So it must have got the better of you.'

'And I hope it goes on doing so in that instance. Figure of speech, boyo, figure of speech.'

'How can fucking someone else's wife be a figure of speech?'

'You mean it feels more like a slip of the tongue? I'm with you there.'

That Friday, when Jack went home to Hampshire, he was more than civilly pleased to see both the country and his wife. The bantams scattered in colourful panic as he turned the car into the drive; the smell of tobacco plants in the limp evening air delighted him; the front door which let in a draught all winter now pleased him with its picturesque inefficiency. Jack didn't fool himself about rural idylls; he just fooled himself about two-day rural idylls.

'There's my sparky,' he said, as Sue came through from the kitchen to greet him. When he hadn't seen her for five days he liked to play up to her vital, dynamic, Irish side; and he congratulated himself on having the guts to marry a woman of character. He ran his eye easily, proprietorially, over her sleek outline, sharp features, dark colouring, and was pleased with what he saw. Part of the ease came from not having anything in particular to feel guilty about; part of the pleasure came from its being Friday. He loved his wife best on Fridays.

Sue, for her part, seemed happy at the start of the weekend. As they sat over steak and kidney pudding at the refectory table, while wood smoke drifted in from the other room, she told him the pump gossip and he responded with news from London.

'And another thing. You know I told you about Graham coming round a few weeks ago?'

'Yes.'

'Well, I had him back. In fact, both the Hendricks came, separately, Graham *and* Ann.' Jack had promised not to talk about their visits, but didn't hesitate. After all, he was so notoriously unreliable that no one in his proper mind would expect him to keep a promise; he wouldn't get any credit for secrecy, would he? Besides, wives didn't count anyway, that was the law, wasn't it?

Sue had looked across at him sharply when he mentioned Ann's name; so he hurried along with his explanation.

'Seems Graham still can't handle her past and old Jack's cast as father confessor.'

'You must enjoy that.'

'I do a bit. Though I don't envy those priests doing it all the time.'

'Well, they've got that book with all the answers, haven't they? Just look it up in the old black book and whatever it is stop doing it.'

Jack chuckled, leaned across and kissed his wife wetly on the temple. He thought she was smart. She thought he was sentimental.

'So what advice did you give?'

'Well, I think I told Ann to take him off on holiday; and I told Graham assorted stuff, but the only thing he seems to have followed is taking up wanking again.'

Sue laughed. She'd never much cared for Ann, always found her a bit flash, a bit too self-contained; didn't make enough mistakes to be human. Flash trash she'd once called her to Jack; but then at the time there were extenuating circumstances. As for Graham, he was nice enough, but a bit … wet, really. Fancy getting upset about the past. There was enough in most people's presents to give you sleepless nights if that's what you were keen on having.

'I don't think you've earned your Solomon badge yet.'

Jack laughed, and dabbed some gravy off his beard.

'And the funny thing was that first I had one of them round consulting me and insisting I didn't tell the other, and then the next day the other came brandishing exactly the same precondition.'

'Sounds like a Whitehall farce. Stop brandishing that precondition at me.'

'And I remember thinking, as I shut the door on Graham the second time,' (what came next was a lie, but Jack was churning with Friday-night sentiment) 'I remember thinking, well, Sue and I have our little rows, and we may have our bad days, but we'd never do anything like *that*.' He leaned across and kissed the frontier of her hair again. She immediately straightened up and began collecting the dishes.

'No, I shouldn't think we would. We'd find a less complicated way to deceive one another, wouldn't we?'

There's my sparky, Jack thought, as he smiled at her departing back. He followed her out to the kitchen and insisted on washing up, just for a change. They went to bed early, and Jack, also for a change, combed his beard in the bathroom beforehand.

After they had made love, he lay on his back quite alert, with Sue tucked sleepily into his shoulder. He found himself thinking about Graham, about how, with a casual remark, a joke even, he'd started him off wanking again after twenty years. Twenty years! Jack envied him that. Well, envied knowing what breaking such a fast felt like.

The next week, one afternoon when Ann was at work, Graham sat in his study addressing the Jiffy bags. The plastic linings crackled as he stuck down the labels he'd typed on the departmental typewriter. He checked the actors' addresses again with his copy of *Spotlight* (most of them were c/o agents, but he thought they'd get through), picked up his stapler and went down to the kitchen.

The butcher had been surprised by his order. Either that Mr Hendrick had fallen on hard times, or else he'd bought himself an expensive dog. The butcher hadn't asked. It sickened him the way he often sold the same cuts both to fretting pensioners and rich dog-owners.

Graham got out the biggest chopping board they had. First he skinned the black pudding and squeezed it out. Then he piled the soft, damp brains on top and began kneading them into the black pudding. As the creamy-pink tissues squelched between his fingers, he found himself remembering what Jack had said. But did that apply to animals as well? Were bits of this stuff prehistoric and other bits more finely developed? He stared at it for a while, but it all seemed to have the same consistency and structure. Maybe the lighter bits were the Four-Eyes, the darker bits the Sawn-Offs. Still, no matter. Then he chopped up the bloated, goose-pimpled ox tongue and mixed that in. It looked disgusting, like a god's vomit; it didn't smell too good either. Graham washed his hands, then smiled to himself as he scooped a quarter of the mixture into each of the Jiffy bags. He washed his hands again, then stapled up the bags. He checked his watch: plenty of time to get to the post office.

# SIX

# *Mister Carwash*

And that was when the sneering dreams began. The dreams which were so strong, and so contemptuous, that they strode carelessly across the barrier of consciousness.

The first one came the night after he'd dropped in at the N.F.T. to check up on his wife's adultery with Buck Skelton. The pudgy, stetsoned, middle-rank American star had once been shipped to London, on a tame producer's whim, to play the part of special marshal from Arizona unexpectedly seconded to Scotland Yard. *The Rattler and the Rubies*, a comedy-thriller now being revived in a season called 'The Clash of Genres', included a brief scene where Ann, playing a cloakroom girl at a fashionable gaming club, indulged in some good-natured banter with a Buck who seemed to move through the sophisticated yet decadent gathering with a marvellous natural dignity.

'Jest here for to put the rec'd straight,' Buck began in confidential tones. 'Always believe in man to man on these occasions.' He was lying on a beach lounger at the edge of his swimming pool; Graham, ridiculously white-skinned, was squatting uncomfortably beside him on a shoe-shiner's stool. A Pina Colada frothed at Buck's elbow; behind him, a girl's naked bottom suddenly broke the surface of the pool like a dolphin, waggled, and disappeared again. The sun was bouncing off the water into Graham's eyes. Buck wore tinted shades whose density adjusted itself according to the brightness of the day; Graham could only just see his eyes.

'Reason ah told you to drop bah,' came the cowboy voice, 'is jest fer to put you in the picture, as the movie producer said as he grabbed the starlet's jugs, her her. Jest wanted to let you know what went on between your lil old lady and this here Buck. Know why they call me Buck? I figger you can guess.

'Now, *Rattler* was a real bitch movie.' He sucked up an inch of Pina Colada through an oval, candy-striped straw. 'A re-al bitch. We had a cokehead director, a couple of fag writers, a screw-up a day with that actors' union of yours. I didn't let it get to me, of course. I'm a pro. That's why I'm still in work. That's why I'll always be in work. The rules are easy, Gray-ham. Number one, always take what your agent offers. Number two, never piss on the script; just say your lines as best you can, even if they are written by a couple of sky-high ass-inspectors. Number three, never get hooched on set. And number fower, don't start balling the leading lady until you know exactly when shooting's gonna stop.' He took off his shades and stared at Graham for a few seconds; then replaced them.

'Now, it was Rule Number Fower that took me by way of your wife. There were these union screw-ups, and to tell the truth I didn't really give shit about that beanbag they'd cast to play my girl pardner, and we jest didn't know how long we'd be sitting around on our butts waiting for the Queen to go by, no disrespect. I'm a pretty manly sort of fellow at the best of times, and when it's the worst of times, well, I guess that jest makes me a sight manlier. Couldn't wait to get the old Rattler into somebody's Rubies, seemed like more than a good idea.'

Graham stared moodily at Buck, taking in the slightly ridged nose, the ox-blood tan, the spurt of hair at the fork of his open shirt. One or two of the hairs seemed to be turning grey, but this only made him more threatening to Graham: he was boastfully adding maturity and wisdom to his obviously colossal virility.

'Now, first time I set eyes on that little Annie of yours, I knew she was gonna prove a real firecracker. "Annie," I says to her, "you play your cards right, and maybe you'll get my gun." Haw haw. Always a little joke like that at the start, something to get them thinking what might come their way. Let them turn it over for a couple of days, then they drop into the palm of your hand like a rahp pay-yaych. That's old Buck's philosophy, any road.

'So, stranger.' The actor suddenly became more business-like, more distant. 'So, I were jest giving her the old couple-of-days' routine, waiting for the sherry wine to matoor in the caysk, so to speak, when she comes right up to me and says, "How's about finding a holster for your gun, cowboy?" So that's what the chicks are like over here, Buck, I says to myself.

'Now, I've known some spirited gals in my time, stranger, but that little Annie ... Back at the hotel she was hustling me outa my duds in the elevator. And then she really took off. Fightin', bitin', scratchin' — I even had to *re-strain* her a bit. The studio might have wanted a tub shot or something, and I jest had to haul her nails outa my back. I hauled them out and slapped her down, but that only seemed to make her wilder, which I s'pose I should have anticipated, so I jest reached across to my pants and slid out my lizard-skin belt and tied her wrists out of harm's way.

'And after that, every time we balled she made me tie her wrists up. Jest seemed to excite her some more. Not that there was much room for more. She was right off that scale, stranger; hurricane force nine was a gentle breeze where she came from.

'But what she really liked me to do — after I'd tied her up, natch — was to chew her ass. You do that to her, stranger? She *let* you do that to her, stranger? I'd get me down there and start eating her out; I mean, it was a carry-out lunch counter as far as I was concerned. Then I'd sorta slide down a bit further, and I'd feel her squirm, and that current went

87

*raht* through her body. Then I'd eat some more, then slide back to her ass. I'd chew it some and diddle my tongue around, and then, when she was all wound up, I'd jest plunge my tongue right in, and when I did that she'd *ex-plode*. Never missed. Bang, like a mousetrap. She used to say, now she understood what a cowpoke was.

'She ever let you do that?' The tone became more taunting. 'Mean to say, I bet you kiss a lot of ass one way and another; but you ever do it for real, stranger? Or does little Annie only let the other fellers do *that* to her? You wouldn't know, would you? That's jest the trouble with you fag fellers. You get all uppity about *unnerstandin'* chicks. Never met a chick yet who wanted to be *unnerstood*—least, not when getting balled flat was the alternative. Still, you carry on *unnerstandin'* the chicks, and I'll carry on ballin' them.'

In the pool behind Buck another shimmering bottom broke the surface. This time it stayed suspended there for a few seconds, and as Graham gawped the buttocks slid wetly apart. Graham, from his shoe-shine stool, looked across at Buck, who stuck out the tip of his tongue and ran it round his lips. Graham hurled himself at Buck, but the cowboy, with a swivel of the hips, made him miss his aim. As Graham lurched past, a Frye boot caught him in the thigh and twisted him into the pool. Though he normally swam strongly, the water proved so viscous that he progressed in slow motion. Eventually, after several minutes, he got both hands on the pool's rim. As he prepared to haul himself out, a shadow fell across his face and a boot was placed firmly on the fingertips of his right hand.

'Say, stranger,' Buck spat down at him, 'you still hanging around my prahpurty? Thought you'd been run out days ago. When I say kiss off, I'm gonna mean kiss off.' And with that he took his glass of Pina Colada and threw the milky froth into Graham's face.

Graham woke up in the dark. The fingertips of his right hand were jammed between the mattress and the base of the bed. He had dribbled on the pillow and his face was wet with his own spit. His pyjamas were twisted tightly round his legs and to his surprise he found he had an erection.

He didn't think she possibly could have. Surely not a tubby, bogus cowboy like that. But how could you know whom your wife might have fancied before she fancied you? For a start, women often succumbed for such odd reasons: like pity, and politeness, and loneliness, and rage at a third party, and, sod it, sheer sexual pleasure. Graham sometimes wished he'd had a go at succumbing for different reasons.

The next day, while his brain officially dealt with Bonar Law, Carson and the Ulster Volunteers, he turned over the question of Buck. Dreams couldn't be true, could they: that was why they were dreams. There were supposed to be premonitory dreams — the wise man sees a vision of floods, and moves his tribe to higher ground; and in his own civilization, didn't you have dreams before job interviews, warning you against making mistakes? So why couldn't you have post-monitory dreams? It was, if anything, a more plausible concept. He could easily have picked up something from Ann at a subliminal level, and then his brain might decide to break the news to him tactfully in his sleep. Why not?

Of course, the Buck of his dream was very different from the Buck of *The Rattler and the Rubies*. In the dream, he'd been a threatening, coarse fellow; in the film, one of nature's prairie gentlemen. Neither image, Graham assumed hopefully, would be particularly alluring to Ann; but then both of them were false images — one on a screen, one in his head. What was the real Buck Skelton like (what was his real n me, for a start)? And maybe that Buck was the one to find favour with Ann.

Baulked, Graham's brain turned, with scarcely any encouragement, to dreams of revenge. First, he drowned the cowboy in a swimming pool of Pina Colada: the final bubbles from Buck's failing lungs went unnoticed among all the froth on the pool's surface. Then he bribed someone to put a rattlesnake in the path of Buck's horse just as he was passing a giant cactus: the stallion reared, Buck was thrown, and as he clutched automatically at the cactus, two giant spines, as strong as steel, drove through his leather chaps and transfixed his balls as if they were cocktail sausages.

The final revenge was the best, though. If there'd been one thing Graham hated, it was the way Buck had used his sunglasses. He disliked people who wore them as proof of character; but he also felt rather primly aggressive towards the glasses themselves. He disapproved of inanimate things taking on a life of their own, trying to organize a fourth estate in the world, after people, animals and plants; it upset him, threatened him even.

He'd once read a motoring column warning drivers against wearing such glasses if their route took them through tunnels: the shifts of light were too sudden for the glasses, which took several seconds to adjust across their full range. Graham was fairly sure that Buck was not a great reader of motoring columns, and would be unprepared for this hazard as he headed north out of L.A. along the coast road. Frisco by nightfall, he'd promised the whore bitch tart splayed out over the front seat of his Coupe de Ville. The radio was tuned to Buck's favourite bluegrass station; on the back seat lay a tray of Coor's beer.

Just north of Big Sur they reached a natural rock tunnel. For a couple of seconds Buck slowed, then his shades readjusted themselves and he picked up speed again. They came out of the tunnel into bright sunshine at sixty miles per hour. Graham hoped Buck would have time to utter a characteristic, 'What in hell's sakes is goin' on here?', but it didn't really matter. Ten yards from the tunnel's mouth the Coupe de Ville smashed into the lowered blade of a thirty-two ton bulldozer. Graham himself sat in the control seat wearing oily denims and a bright yellow hardhat. A spurt of flame appeared above the top edge of the bulldozer's blade, followed by Buck's body, which hurtled high over Graham's cabin. He looked round, kicked the dozer into reverse gear, and trundled slowly over the lifeless body, mashing its bones and rolling the flesh out as thin as pastry. He put the dozer back into forward drive, pushed the wreckage of the Coupe de Ville off the side of the road and heard it bounce down towards the Pacific. Then, with a final glance over his shoulder at the scarlet pastry-man on the road, he clanked back down the tunnel.

'Can I ask you someone else?' Graham said as they lay in bed the next night.

'Of course.' Ann braced herself. She hoped it would be better than last time; and the time before.

'Buck Skelton.'

'Buck Skelton? Christ, what have you seen? I can't remember acting with him.'

'*The Rattler and the Rubies.* Bloody terrible it was too. You played the cloakroom girl who takes the hero's stetson and says, "My, we don't normally get such big ones in here".'

'I said *that*?' Ann was interested, as well as relieved. She also felt a stab of indignation at the misplaced accusation. If he thinks I might have fucked *Skelton*, who wouldn't he suspect? For once, Ann decided to let Graham wait for his reassurance.

'Afraid so,' he replied. 'You gave every word its full weight.'

'And what did he say back?'

'Don't remember. Some balls about the red meat they eat in Arizona making everything grow bigger. Something subtle like that.'

'And what did I say to that?'

'You didn't. That was your only line. You just looked dreamy.'

'Yes, I remember having to do that often enough. My goosed-with-a-warm-glove look.' She felt Graham tense at

the phrase. 'The way I did it was to concentrate very hard
on the last really good meal I'd had. It would make my eyes
come over all misty with lust.'

'So?'

The body beside her was tensing itself again.

'So?'

'So did you go to bed with him?'

'Did I fuck Buck Skelton? Graham, Gabby Hayes would
have had more chance.'

Graham turned towards her and pressed his face against
her upper arm; his hand reached across and laid itself on her
stomach.

'Though I did let him kiss me once.'

His suggestion had been so ludicrous that she thought he
was due total honesty in return. She felt Graham's hand
stiffen on her stomach. She sensed he was still waiting.

'On the cheek. He kissed everyone goodbye – all the girls,
that is. The ones that would let him, on the lips; the ones
that wouldn't, on the cheek.'

Graham grunted in the dark, then gave a victor's satisfied
chuckle. Approximately three minutes later he started making love to Ann. He was thorough and affectionate, but she
kept her mind elsewhere. If she had in fact fucked Skelton,
she was thinking, Graham wouldn't be making love to me
now. How strange the ways in which the past caught up and
tugged at the present. What if, all those years ago, when she
was making *The Rattler and the Rubies*, someone had said, 'Let
that cowboy have his way with you and some years from now
you'll give yourself, and a man you don't even know, a night
or two of guaranteed misery.' What if someone had said
that? As likely as anything, she'd have said, Fuck the future.
FUCK THE FUTURE. Get off my back; you'll cause enough
bother when you arrive without fucking me around beforehand. And then, to make the point, she might have just gone
ahead and smiled at the cowboy, plump and vain as he was.

Graham was getting more excited, pushing her legs out at

a more open angle and sliding his hand flat underneath her shoulders. He'd even tensed up when she'd mentioned a farewell kiss on the cheek. If Skelton had kissed her on the lips all those years ago, would that have been enough to stop Graham making love to her tonight? It seemed a strange equation to make. Why were there so many unguessable connections around like this? And what if you ever were able to guess them all in advance: would that stop life turning nasty on you? Or would it find some other way?

Graham held off his climax for a bit, tacitly offering her the chance to come if she wanted to. She felt no temptation, so answered by pulling rhythmically on his buttocks. As he came, she felt compassion and reflected excitement, as usual, but more distantly.

And the same night, Graham had the carwash dream.

The carwash dream was compèred by Larry Pitter, with whom Ann committed adultery in *The Rumpus*, a street-gang movie Graham had managed to catch twice in the last few months, once at the ABC Turnpike Lane and once out at Romford. Ann played 'Third Gang Girl' and appeared in several inept mood-setting scenes where the gang members strutted and pranced before their greasy harem. Larry Pitter played the detective sergeant who, having beaten up not quite enough suspects to get at the truth, finally bed-bullies Third Gang Girl into splitting on her mates.

Pitter sat behind his desk smoking; he was still wearing his soiled cream Burberry from the film.

'Well, well,' he began with a sneering curiosity, 'look what the moggie's returned with. Hey, boys,' he shouted past Graham, who was seated in the suspect's chair, 'Hey, boys, come see.'

The door opened and three men walked in. Each in his different way struck Graham as dirty and malign. There was the tall young one with straggling greasy hair and acne; the fat, surly one in a stained boiler-suit; and the lean, expressionless one with a two-day growth of beard, who looked like a photofit picture. They should all have been in the cells; but Pitter welcomed them.

'Look, boys, look what's turned up—it's Mister Carwash himself.'

The boys sniggered, and clustered round Pitter on the other side of the desk.

'I think I've got some explaining to do,' said the detective. 'No point beating about the bush, squire, is there?' Graham rather wished they would beat about the bush. 'The thing is, Graham—don't mind if I call you Graham, do you?—thing is, I dare say you've heard a little bit about me from your lady wife. Correct me if I'm wrong.'

Graham didn't speak.

'Told you about our little fling. Our bit of extra-curricular. Very fine thing, a bit of honesty between husband and wife, I always say. I'm sure your marriage is the envy of most of your friends, Graham.'

Pitter gave an insincere, teeth-together smile; Graham didn't comment.

'Course, there is such a thing as too much honesty, isn't there? I mean, what's more important, Graham, your husband's good opinion of you, or telling everything just exactly like it was? Tricky one that, isn't it?

'Anyway, I'm sure Ann did quite the right thing at the time. Told you about me, didn't tell you why we called her the Carwash Girl.' The three villains behind him chuckled. 'Now, stop me if I'm boring you, Graham, but you see, what she really liked wasn't just me. It was all of us. All of us at the same time. Doing different things to her. I won't be specific, I know these things can be hurtful; I'll just leave you to imagine it. But the first time she got us all to do things to her at the same time, we were all sort of swarming over her, licking her and stuff, she said it was just like being in a carwash. So we called her the Carwash Girl. And we used to giggle about what would happen when she met Mister Right. Only we used to call *him* Mister Carwash. I mean, she

94

made it quite plain that it was the more the merrier as far as she was concerned. And how would any husband cope with that, we wondered. Unless, of course, there's more to you than meets the eye.' Pitter grinned.

'But anyway,' he went on, taking an avuncular tone, 'women change. They do, don't they? Maybe she'll get back to liking one fellow at a time. Then you won't need to feel so inadequate, will you? Won't need to feel that however good you are she'll always be dreaming of that extra oomph. You never can tell, it might work out like that. So what I'm really saying, Mister Carwash, is that the boys and me wish you the best of British. We really do. We think you've drawn a pretty short straw, and we just hope you manage to play your cards right.'

Then all four of them leaned across the desk and shook him by the hand. He didn't want to accept any of the outstretched palms which had once caressed the racked body of his wife, but found himself unable to draw back. The men seemed full of sympathy for him; one of them even winked.

What if it were true? Graham had woken up in a silent, taut-muscled panic. What if it were true? It couldn't be true. He knew Ann too well. They'd even—haltingly—discussed their sexual fantasies with each other, and she'd never mentioned *that*. But then, of course, if she'd already done it, it wouldn't be a fantasy any more, would it? No, it couldn't be true. But what if it referred to a sort of truth? Did he feel confident that he satisfied her? No. Yes. No. Yes. Don't know. Well, what about tonight, for instance—that was all for you, wasn't it? Yes, but there's no rule that you both have to come every time, is there? Of course not, but she didn't exactly seem overwhelmed by your caresses, did she? No, but that's all right, too. It may be *all right*, you may have talked about it and agreed it was *all right*, but that's not how sex works, is it? It's where the unsayable is king; it's where madness and surprise rule; it's where the cheques you write for ecstasy are drawn on the bank of despair.

Graham slowly debated himself to sleep again.

But Larry Pitter, as he might have guessed, didn't go away with waking up. He hung around in some back alley of Graham's brain, a half-seen figure slouched against a lamp-post, taking his time, smoking a fag, ready to saunter out and trip Graham up when he felt like it.

Graham decided to drive to work that morning; he had only two hours' teaching and could leave the car on a meter. As he set off, rain began spotting the windscreen. He turned on his wipers, then his washers, then his car radio. Something bracing and carefree emerged; perhaps it was a Rossini string sonata. He felt a surge of gratitude, a paperback historian's thrill, for living at this particular time. Easy travel, protection from the weather, button culture: Graham suddenly felt as if all such benefits had only just arrived, as if only yesterday he'd been a berry-eater on Box Hill who ran for cover at the gentlest goat's bray.

He drove past a garage on the opposite side of the road:

FOUR STAR
THREE STAR
TWO STAR
DERV
CARDS
TOILETS
CARWASH

and the day was gone, destroyed. Larry Pitter had sidled out of his alley and slyly removed a manhole cover; Graham, head up, whistling, feeling the sun on his face, had walked straight into it.

The Rossini continued but Graham thought only of Ann lying on her back encouraging the four men. They were lined up side by side at right angles to her body, each licking a swath, like four motor mowers moving over her. Graham shook his head to expel the image, and concentrated on

96

driving; but the picture, though rebuked and diminished, continued mockingly at the edge of his vision, up in the rear-view mirror.

He found himself watching the road for garages. At each he instinctively flicked an eye down the rows of signs, looking for the one that said CARWASH. Mostly, they didn't; and each one that didn't made Graham feel elated, as if all his suspicions of adultery had been proved false. Then he would pass the eighth or ninth garage, with its contemptuously informative sign, and the image in the rear-view mirror would sharpen. Now, he could see his wife urging the four men to make their different uses of her. Three took the obvious channels; the fourth squatted in the corner of the mirror like a distempered satyr and pulled on his cock. Graham forced his attention back to the road. The rain had slackened off, and with every sweep the wipers were now depositing some of their own dirt back on the screen. Automatically, Graham reached out and pressed the windscreen washer. A burst of bubbly opaque liquid hit the glass in front of his face. He should have known better. Up in the mirror the satyr was coming.

Graham spent twenty minutes of his first class looking at his male students and wondering if any of them wanted to go into films and commit adultery with his wife. Then this struck even him as comical, and he went back to expounding a tentatively revisionist view of Balfour. After a couple of hours he emerged, walked to his car, and gazed at the windscreen washer nozzles on the bonnet as if they were instruments of adultery. An enervating sadness began to creep through him. He bought a racing edition of the *Evening Standard* and checked through the films. Maybe he should see something that didn't have his wife in for a change. What about the new Jancso not starring his wife, the new intergalactic battleorama not starring his wife, or the new British road movie about hitch-hiking to Wrexham, definitely not starring his wife?

97

Not a single one of his wife's films was showing. Not one. Graham felt as if a branch of the social services which particularly affected him had suddenly been withdrawn. Did they realize the effects of their cuts? He couldn't, today, go to any cinema in London or its immediate suburbs and see a film in which his wife committed adultery; nor could he see any film in which his wife, though remaining chaste on-screen, had committed adultery offscreen with one of the actors. The two categories, he noticed, were beginning to get blurred in his head.

That left two further categories of film he could still catch up on: other films featuring actors with whom his wife had committed adultery onscreen (but not off); and other films featuring actors with whom his wife had committed adultery offscreen (but not on). He checked through the *Evening Standard* again. This time the choice was limited to two: Rick Fateman in *Sadismo* at Muswell Hill (on but not off); or Larry Pitter in a remake of *The Sleeping Tiger* ... Graham suddenly realized that he couldn't remember whether or not Ann actually had committed adultery with Pitter. Onscreen, yes, of course, that was what had driven him, turbulent with jealousy, to Turnpike Lane and Romford in the last few days. But offscreen? He knew he'd asked her, months ago, but found he simply couldn't remember the answer. This struck him as very strange.

Maybe *The Sleeping Tiger* would help him out. He drove to Swiss Cottage in a state of vivid curiosity. In the remake, Pitter played the psychiatrist who brings home a green-haired girl punk and employs her as an au pair; the girl seduces his wife, tries to rape his ten-year-old son, slashes his cats' throats with a razor, and then unexpectedly returns home to her mother. The wife has a nervous breakdown and the husband discovers he is homosexual. A sort of truth is attained through the experience of deep pain. The young English director displayed his homage to the early, pseudonymous Losey with several caressing shots of banisters and staircases. Pitter at one point attempted to dally with the object of his research and, to Graham's delight, received a swift kick in the balls.

Graham came out of the cinema as excited as he had gone in. Realizing that he didn't know whether or not Ann *had* committed adultery with Pitter made him feel keenly alive. As he drove home, one or two methods of killing Pitter sauntered into his head, but he dismissed them as idle fantasies. What he was on to now was much more important, much more real.

At home, he carefully stabbed the steaks and poked pieces of garlic into the incisions. He laid the table, adding candlesticks at the last moment. He got out the rarely-used ice bucket and broke some ice into it for Ann's gin and tonic. He was whistling as she opened the front door. When she walked into the dining-room he kissed her unambiguously on the lips and handed her a drink, followed by a bowl of shelled pistachio nuts. He hadn't been like this for weeks.

'Has something happened?'

'No, nothing special.' But he looked a little furtive as he said it. Maybe something had happened at work; maybe Alice had done well at school; maybe he just felt unaccountably better. All through dinner he remained in good spirits. Then, over coffee, he finally said,

'What happened today hasn't happened before.' He sounded as if he were slowly unwrapping a present for Ann. 'Never before. It was most instructive.' He smiled at her with puzzling gentleness. 'I forgot whether or not you'd gone to bed with Larry Pitter.' He looked across at her, expecting approval.

'So?' Ann felt her stomach beginning to contract with apprehension.

'So. So, it's never happened before. Every one of ... of the others I've always remembered. Everyone you ... fucked.' He used the word with deliberation. 'Whether you did it on or off. Even when you did it neither, like with Buck Skelton.

99

Every minute of the day, if someone stopped me and said, "Give me a list of all the other men your wife has fucked," I could do so. I really could. And then I'd say, "And there are some more, the other categories." I could remember all those as well, all of them. I once found myself automatically marking up a student simply because he was called Kerrigan —because Jim Kerrigan never made a pass at you in *The Cheapest Place in Town*.'

Ann strained a smile through her face and waited.

'So what this may mean is that I'm beginning to forget.'

'Yes, I suppose it may.' But Graham looked excited rather than relieved, she thought.

'Go on then.'

'Go on what?'

'Test me.'

'Test you?'

'Yes. See how much I remember. "Have I fucked so-and-so?", that sort of thing. "Who played the second male lead in what film whom I fucked onscreen but not off?" Go on, it sounds like a good game.'

'Are you drunk?' Maybe he'd had a few before she got home.

'Not at all. Not in the least.' He certainly didn't look it: he looked bright, cheerful, happy.

'Then all I can say is I think it's the sickest suggestion I've ever heard.'

'Oh, come on. Be a sport. Homo ludens, etcetera.'

'You are serious, aren't you?'

'I'm serious about playing games, yes.'

Ann said quietly, 'I think you're mad.'

Graham didn't seem at all put out.

'No, I'm not mad. I just find it all very interesting. I mean, I was so surprised today, when I couldn't remember, that I went off to see *The Sleeping Tiger*.'

'What's that?'

'What do you mean? It's Larry Pitter's last film but one.'

'Why should I be interested in Larry Pitter's films?'

'Because he didn't, or as the case may be, did, fuck you; definitely onscreen in *The Rumpus*, and offscreen, well, that's what this is all about.'

'You went to see some film with Pitter in it?' Ann was amazed; appalled. 'Why?'

'*The Sleeping Tiger*. To see if it would jog my memory.'

'Ah. On locally, was it?'

'Swiss Cottage.'

'Graham, that's miles out of anyone's way. All for some crappy film with Pitter in it. You must be crazy.'

Graham wasn't in the least deterred. He looked across at his wife with unequivocal tenderness.

'Wait, wait. The point was, I sat all the way through *The Sleeping Tiger* and at the end I was still no nearer remembering. I looked at Larry Pitter's face every time it came on the screen and I simply couldn't remember whether or not I wanted to kill him. It was very odd.'

'Well, I suppose if it makes you feel better in some way, that's a start.'

Graham paused, then said slowly,

'I don't know about better.' Ann was getting more and more lost. 'No, I wouldn't say better. I'd say different. It's a new twist, you see. And I'm wondering why, if my brain chose to forget one of them, it should pick on Larry Pitter. What's Pitter got, or not got, that the others haven't?'

'Graham, I think this is worrying. I've always been able to understand you before. Now I can't. It used to upset you when we talked about my old boyfriends. It always upsets me. Now it just ... it just seems to excite you in some way.'

'Only this Pitter business. It's as if I hadn't ever known in the first place. It's really as if I'm about to discover for the first time whether or not you've fucked Larry Pitter.'

'You're serious. You're bloody serious, aren't you?'

Graham leaned across the dinner table and gently took Ann's wrist.

'Did you?' he said quietly, as if a louder voice would disturb the answer. 'Did you?'

Ann pulled away her arm. She had never imagined that Graham would provoke in her the disgusted pity she now felt.

'You don't think I'm going to tell you, do you; now?' she replied, equally softly.

'Why not? I need to know. I've got to know.' His eyes had the brightness of fever in them.

'*No*, Graham.'

'Come on, love. You've told me before. Just tell me again.'

'*No*.'

'You've told me before.' The soft voice, the excited eyes, the hand back again on her wrist, only this time more firmly.

'Graham, I've told you before and you've forgotten so it can't bother you that much whether I did or didn't.'

'I need to know.'

'No.'

'I need to *know*.'

Ann tried a last appeal to reason, and a last attempt to suppress her own anger.

'Look, either I didn't or I did. If I didn't then it doesn't matter; if I did and you've forgotten, then that's the same as me not having done so in the first place, isn't it? If you don't remember, it doesn't matter, so let's say I didn't.'

Graham merely repeated, more insistently,

'I need to know.'

Ann tried to pull her wrist away without success, then took a deep breath.

'Of course I did. I enjoyed it. He was a great screw. I asked him to bugger me as well.'

The grasp relaxed at once. Graham's eyes went dull. He looked down in front of him.

They didn't speak again all evening. They sat in separate rooms and then went to bed without consulting one another.

As Ann was coming out of the bathroom—she had locked the door for once—Graham was waiting to go in. He stood further aside than was needed to let her pass.

In bed, they lay with their backs to one another, a yard of space between them. In the dark, Graham began to cry quietly. After a few minutes Ann began to cry too. Finally she said,

'It wasn't true.'

Graham stopped crying for the moment, and she repeated, 'It wasn't true.'

Then they both began crying again, still curled away on the edges of the bed.

# SEVEN

# *On the Dunghill*

Italy was out for a start: it was criss-crossed with lovers' footprints, like camel tracks in a desert where the wind never blew. Germany and Spain were sort of half-out. There were some countries — Portugal, Belgium, Scandinavia — which were completely safe; though one of the reasons for this, of course, was that Ann had never wanted to go there in the first place. So this 'safeness' was in its turn dangerous: craven though Graham was inclined to be, the idea of being bullied into a fortnight in Helsinki by the absent presences of Benny and Chris and Lyman and whoever didn't appeal. He imagined himself in one of those fringe countries, anoraked against the cold and sipping a glass of goat's-hoof liquor; all there would be to do was brood chippily on the easy, sun-tanned shits who had driven him there and who were even now lolling down the Via Veneto and mocking the thought of him.

France was semi-dangerous. Paris was out; the Loire was out; the South was out. Well, not all the South: only those flash bits where the curving cliffs have been replaced by curving terraces of flats, the Nice and Cannes bits where Ann, he imagined, had behaved as ... as any other girl would. But of course there was the 'real' South, where neither of them had been, nor had those posh studs who were always telephoning London to check the movement of their port-folios. The real South: that was safe.

They flew to Toulouse, hired a car, and for no particular

reason other than that it was one of the offered directions out of the city, followed the Canal du Midi south-east to Carcassonne. They had clambered halfway round the ramparts before some remark of Ann's made Graham break the news to her that it was all Viollet-le-Duc's restoration; but this didn't diminish her enjoyment. She was determined, as far as determination would carry her, to enjoy the holiday. Graham disliked Carcassonne intensely—no doubt because of historian's integrity, he explained half-jokingly to Ann—but this didn't matter. On the first day of their drive he'd been nervous, anxiously keen to escape the paternal fascination with his responses of Benny, Chris, Lyman and the others; by now, though, he seemed to have left them behind.

Narbonne offered a T-junction; they turned north, up through Béziers and into the Hérault. On the fourth morning, driving carefully through an alley of fat plane trees, each with a fading band of white around its midriff, Graham slowed to pass an overflowing haycart; and as the driver, apparently asleep, shifted his head half-sideways at them and tugged lethargically on the reins, he suddenly felt that everything inside him was almost as good as it had been at the beginning. That evening, he lay under a single sheet in the hotel bed and stared at the peeling whitewash on the ceiling; it reminded him of the peeling band of insect-deterrent round the plane trees, and he smiled again to himself. They couldn't get him here; none of them had ever been here before, so they wouldn't know where to look; and even if they could find him, now, tonight, he'd be strong enough to chase them away.

'What are you smiling at?'

Ann, naked, a pair of rinsed-out knickers in her hand, was hovering by the window, wondering whether to hang them over the wrought-iron railing outside. Eventually she decided against it: the next day was a Sunday, and you never could tell what people judged to be blasphemous.

'Just smiling.' He took off his glasses and laid them on the bedside table.

She hung her knickers on the projecting snout of the radiator, and walked across towards the bed. Graham always looked so much more defenceless without his glasses. She looked at the indentations on his nose; then at his patchily greying hair; then at the whiteness of his flesh. One of the first things he'd said to her that had made her laugh was, 'I'm afraid I've got an academic's body.' She remembered this as she slipped in under the sheet.

'Just smiling?'

Graham had already decided that for the next however many days he would avoid all references to what they had come on holiday partly to forget. So instead he told her something that had made him smile the night before.

'I was thinking about an indicative thing.'

'Uh-huh?' She pushed towards him and laid her hand on his academic chest.

'Towards the end of, of my time with Barbara, do you know what she used to do to me? It's all right, it won't make you cross. She used to plant bedclothes on me. She did, really. While I was asleep she used to pull out the sheets and blankets from her side of the bed and push them over to mine, and then give me all the eiderdown as well, and then pretend to wake up and bollock me for stealing all the bedclothes.'

'That's crazy. Why did she do it?'

'Make me feel guilty, I suppose. It always worked, too. I mean, she used to make me feel that even when I was asleep I was subconsciously trying to give her a rotten deal. She used to do that about once a month for a whole year.'

'Why did she stop?'

'Oh, because I caught her. I was wide awake one night, just lying there, trying not to disturb her. After an hour or so she woke up, but I didn't feel like saying anything to her, so I just stayed quiet. And then I realized what she was doing. So I waited for her to pile everything up on top of me, and then pretend to be asleep, and then pretend to wake up, and then pretend to be cold, and then shake me and start bollocking me, and I just said, "I've been awake for at least an hour." She stopped in mid-sentence, and grabbed back the bedclothes she'd just given me, and turned over. I think it was the only time I can remember when she was at a loss for words.'

Ann pressed her hand down on Graham's chest. She liked the way he talked about his past. He never slanged Barbara just so that she, Ann, would feel better. His stories were always tinged with incredulity at the way he had behaved himself, or had allowed Barbara to behave towards him; and it seemed to imply that such ploys and deceptions didn't, couldn't take place between the two of them.

'Do you want some more sheet?' she asked, and crawled astride him. From the way he smiled up at her she guessed there would be no hesitancies, no rowdy past between them on this occasion. She was right.

They found a small hotel near Clermont l'Hérault and stayed there for a week. At dinner a wide-shouldered litre of local red wine stood on their table, and the chips had a saffron colour and a softness which they thought of as importantly French. Perhaps the colour did come from using exhausted cooking oil; but no matter.

In the mornings they would drive past scrubby vineyards to neighbouring villages, where they would look at churches which somehow made themselves more interesting than they really were, and then spend a lingering time buying picnic material and a copy of *Midi-Libre*. They'd drive a little, rather aimlessly, stopping occasionally for Ann to gather wild flowers and weeds, none of whose names she knew, and which were mostly left to curl and fade on the back shelf of the car. They'd find a bar, have an aperitif, then look for a sheltered slope or a clearing.

Over lunch Graham would get Ann to read him page two of *Midi-Libre*. It was headed *Faits Divers* and specialized in stories of everyday violence. The odder crimes found their niche here, alongside case histories of ordinary people who had simply cracked. 'Distrait mother drives into canal,' Ann would translate, 'five perish.' One day it was a story about a peasant family who kept their octogenarian grandmother chained to her bed 'for fear she might wander to the main route and occasion an accident'; the main route being eight miles away. The next day it was a story about two motorists arguing over a parking space; the loser had taken out a gun and shot his 'enemy of five minutes' three times in the chest. The victim had fallen to the ground; the assailant, for good measure, shot out two of his car tyres before driving off. 'The police continue the pursuit,' Ann translated, 'the victim was gravely blessed and transported to hospital.' Where, Graham thought, he might have to be gravely blessed one more, final time.

'It's all this Latin temperament about,' he said.

'This was in Lille.'

'Ah.'

After lunch they'd drive back to the hotel, have coffee at the bar and then go upstairs to bed. At five o'clock they came down and sat in lurching recliners made of plastic macaroni until it was time for the first drink of the evening. Ann was re-reading *Rebecca*; Graham was on several books at the same time. Occasionally, he would read bits out to her.

> When Pierre Clergue wanted to know me carnally, he used to wear this herb wrapped up in a piece of linen, about an ounce long and wide, or about the size of the first joint of my little finger. And he had a long cord which he used to put round my neck when we made love; and this thing or herb at the end of the cord used to hang down between my breasts, as far as the opening of my stomach. When the priest wanted to get up and

leave the bed, I would take the thing from around my neck and give it back to him. It might happen that he wanted to know me carnally twice or more in a single night; in that case the priest would ask me, before uniting his body with mine, 'Where is the herb?'

'*When* was that?'

'About 1300. Just down the road from here; well, fifty miles or so.'

'Dirty old priest.'

'The priests do seem to have been the randiest. I suppose they could give you absolution afterwards and save you the walk.'

'Dirty old priest.' Ann was shocked by the thought of ecclesiastical carnality. This intrigued Graham: normally it was he who was shocked when she casually told him about the ways of the world. He felt proprietorial, almost malicious, as he continued:

'They didn't all do it. Some of them preferred boys. Not that they were queer or anything—though I suppose they must have been a bit queer. There are lots of passages where men confess things like, "When I was a boy the priest took me into his bed and used me between his thighs as if I were a woman."'

'That sounds pretty queer to me.'

'No; the main reason they had boys was because they didn't want to risk the diseases they might catch from prostitutes.'

'The sods. The fucking sods. And I suppose they made that all right for themselves as well?'

'Oh yes. They made everything all right for themselves. The rule about prostitutes was very interesting. I'll read you it.' He flicked back a few pages. ' "Vidal believed"—he wasn't a priest, he was a muleteer, but this is the conclusion he came to after asking priests about the sins involved in going to prostitutes—"Vidal believed the sexual act to be innocent when performed with a prostitute" ... der der der ... "on two conditions: first, it had to be a monetary transaction" (the man paying, of course); "secondly, the act in question had to 'please' both parties." '

'What does "please" mean? Did the prostitute have to come or something?'

'It doesn't say. I didn't know they knew about coming then.'

Ann reached across from her lounger and poked Graham's leg with her toe. 'They've always known about coming.'

'I thought they only found out about it this century. I thought the Bloomsbury Group discovered coming.' He wasn't entirely joking.

'I think they've always known.'

'Anyway, I shouldn't think "please" necessarily means "come". Probably just means that the client wasn't allowed to hurt the prostitute or beat her up, just as he wasn't allowed to run off without paying.'

'Terrific.'

'Of course,' Graham went on, enjoying himself more as he sensed Ann's distaste growing, 'it probably wasn't much like it is today. I mean, they didn't always do it in bed.'

'Nor do we,' Ann replied automatically, then remembered with alarm that with Graham they always had; it was with, well, some of the others that the location had been movable. Graham, happily, was beyond noticing.

'Where they did it a lot,' he said, delivering his saved-up detail, 'was on dunghills.'

'Dunghills? Errrrruuuukkk.'

'Dunghills. Well, I suppose one can see the advantages.' Graham affected his most academic tone. 'They're warm, they're comfortable, they probably didn't smell much worse than the couple on top of them ...'

'Stop, stop. Enough,' Ann interrupted firmly, 'enough.'

Graham chuckled, and turned back to his book. Ann did the same, though her mind continued with the conversation.

She was surprised at how shocked she felt. Not at single things — the queer priests, the cynical absolutions, the V.D., the dunghills; but at their accumulation. When she'd said that women had always known about coming, she didn't know on what authority she'd spoken; it just seemed that way to her. They must have known, mustn't they: that was the sole force of her argument, she now realized. And in the same way she'd also always assumed, and on no stronger evidence, that sex had always been like it was now. Of course some things had changed — they'd invented the pill and the coil, thank God — but she'd imagined sex as a human constant, as something which was never not refreshing and enjoyed. She associated it in her mind with clean sheets and flowers by the bed. Whereas, not all that long ago, and just down the road, it was dunghills and dirty old priests, and instead of flowers beside you it was dried herbs up you. Why, she wondered, did anyone want to do it under such circumstances? Why did they bother? She wouldn't have. Suddenly, she thought about toothpaste.

Meanwhile Graham read on. It was strange that nowadays he had exactly the same reaction to every history book he read, regardless of length, quality, usefulness or price: he found it at the same time, and almost in the same sentence, intensely interesting and intensely boring.

There were four days of their holiday left when, one morning, Ann felt the skin on her breasts begin to tauten; felt too the first distant ache at the hollow of her back. As they ate their picnic by a flat, wide stream, where the water, never reaching a depth of more than a foot, flowed listlessly over fat pebbles, she murmured to Graham, using the French slang she'd once taught him,

'I think the redcoats are about to land.'

Graham held a long slice of thickly pâtéed bread in his right hand, and in his left a tomato which he'd just bitten into; he knew the juice was currently deciding whether to fall on his trousers, or run up his forearm, or perhaps do both. So it was with only half a mind that he asked,

'Have they just been spotted?'

'Yes.'

'So they're still some way out to sea?'

'Yes.'

'Though of course they may have a following wind?'

'That's always possible.'

He nodded to himself with a sort of private calculation, like a dealer at an auction preview deciding what he'll bid up to. Ann was amused by his responses to the arrival of her periods. Sometimes there would be a long, multiple-choice catechism about precisely where the redcoats had been spotted, what their estimated strength was, how long their expeditionary force planned to stay, and so on. Sometimes, as now, the news seemed to take him quite seriously, as if she'd announced that she had to go into hospital. Occasionally it made him roguishly sexual, and while he wouldn't exactly drag her off to bed—he'd never be that type—he would respond more keenly than usual to encouragement.

To Graham the whole subject was of vivid interest, because for him it was only four years old, and had never before been allowed a sexual slant. He still remained invincibly fastidious about the idea of mid-menstrual sex; he'd even confessed, sheepishly and vaguely, that the thought of it made him feel he ought to be wearing galoshes. But he always agreed readily enough with Ann's suggestion that the imminence of her period meant that it was, well, almost one's duty to allow oneself some quick felicity before close-down. Ann had, once, gone further, and suggested that even if he didn't care to contemplate galoshes, he could always try something a bit different. But Graham didn't really fancy something a bit different; it made him feel awkward, both too bestial and too cerebral at the same time.

During his first marriage it had never been like this. Barbara regarded the arrival of her periods as a time when women's suffering should be exalted, when she should be allowed an extra degree of irrationality in decision-taking, when Graham should be made to feel as guilty as possible. Sometimes he found himself half-thinking that he actually caused Barbara's periods; that it was his penis which had cut her and made her bleed. Certainly it was a time of uncertain temper and strange accusations. Charity suggested that the difference between Barbara's attitude and Ann's could be ascribed to generation, or pain thresholds; but Graham was less tempted by charity nowadays.

When they got back to their hotel after lunch Graham seemed preoccupied; he scarcely spoke as they sipped at their small, chunky, square-handled cups of coffee. Ann didn't ask what he was thinking, but gave him an option.

'Would you like to go for a walk this afternoon?'

'Oh, no, definitely not.'

'Shall I fetch our books?'

'Oh, no, definitely not.'

He leaned across and peered into her cup, checking that it was empty; then stood up. For Graham, this was decisive, almost pushy. They walked upstairs side by side to their bedroom, where the sheets had been pulled so tight and smoothed down so thoroughly that it seemed as if they must be fresh. The room was in an easy darkness, with windows and shutters closed. Graham opened the windows, releasing into the room a faint hum of insects, distant kitchen clatter and the background rumble of a warm afternoon; he left the shutters closed. Perhaps he had been at the window for longer than he realized, for when he turned Ann was already in bed, one arm thrown up on the pillow beside her head, the other automatically holding the sheet half over her breasts. Graham walked round to his side of the bed and sat down, then undressed at moderate pace. The last thing he took off was his glasses, which he placed on the bedside table next to the glass of wilting and mostly unnamable flowers that Ann had collected one morning.

She was unprepared for what followed. First, Graham burrowed down the bed and practically butted her legs apart. Then he began kissing her, with obvious tenderness but no very profitable sense of location. Which was hardly a surprise, since it was only the second time he'd done this. She had assumed she didn't taste nice down there; or at any rate, not nice to him.

Next he reared up, and squirmed his body aggressively sideways, expecting reciprocation. She consented, again with surprise, as she thought he only half-liked that. After about a minute, he scuttled down the bed and pushed inside her, holding his cock as he did so, which was unusual, since he normally liked her to do that for him. And even then he kept moving her about—on her side, on her front, finally, to her relief, on her back—in a diligent, programmed way that hinted at some deeper or more complicated motive than pleasure. It seemed like an act not directly of sex, but of sexual recapitulation. Do it all, do it now, do everything; you never know when you'll do anything, even the simplest kiss, ever again. That was what it seemed to be saying.

And he came differently, too. Whereas his head would usually be buried in the pillow as he rummaged his way breathily to orgasm, this time he reared away from the bed into a press-up, and stared at Ann's face with a seriousness bordering on pain. His expression was both searching and anonymous—he might have been a customs officer to whom she had just offered her passport.

'Sorry,' he said, as his head collapsed back into the pillow beside her. It was the first word he had spoken since they'd been in the bar. He meant, Sorry it didn't work, Sorry for me, Sorry I tried everything and got very little. Sorry for me.

'What for, silly?' She laid a hand across his back and stroked his shoulder.

'All for me. Not enough for you.' But mainly, not enough for me.

'Silly. It's just as nice for me even if I don't.'

Well, it was true often enough for it not to be too much of a lie on this occasion. Graham grunted, as if happy; Ann shifted slightly to reposition his hipbone; and they lay in that traditional posture until the pressure on her bladder became too much.

The next day the redcoats landed, and the weather seemed to shift into greyness. They set off back towards Toulouse, this time following a northern curve. The naves of damp plane trees were planted closer together here, and went *schwaa schwaa* at them as they drove along. The peeling distemper of their barks now made them look run-down: poor-boy trees.

Heading into the southern fringe of the Causses, they saw a sign to Roquefort-sur-Soulzon. Neither of them was much interested in cheese, but this seemed as good a direction as any. They visited a factory cut into a cliff face, where a small female bullfighter wearing three sweaters and a long woollen cape explained to them how the vertical fissures in the rock kept the whole factory at its constant chilly temperature. The breeze and humidity produced unrepeatably perfect conditions for blue cheese making; and also produced, no doubt, the streaming cold of the guide.

There was nothing much for them to see, it transpired, because the cheese making was seasonal, and they had come a little late. There was not even a cheese for them to see: but to compensate, the guide took a large wooden block, carved to the exact size of a whole Roquefort, and demonstrated how to wrap it in tinfoil. The lack of anything to see put Graham in an unshakably good mood, which was increased by Ann's running translation.

'The history goes that there was a berger once who was with his muttons and it was the lunch. He sat in a cavern with some bread and some cheese, when a bergère who was naturally very beautiful passed. The young berger forgot his lunch and made his court to the young bergère. It was a few weeks later when he went back to his cavern that he discovered his cheese all green and his bread all green. But, happily for us, he gusted his cheese and it pleased him much. Then the bergers maintained the secret of the cavern over many centuries. It is not known whether this account is the truth, but it is one the Roqueforties amuse themselves to narrate to one another.'

They walked through several fissures, damp and gleaming with moss of an unnaturally bright green, and were shown, through a window, a distant assembly line of disconsolate packers. The guide announced that the visit was terminating itself, and pointed sternly at a notice which forbade tipping. At the sales counter they disregarded the cheese and resisted a set of twelve colour transparencies of the cheese-making process from mould-collecting to packing. Instead, Graham bought a Roquefort knife: broad-bladed and swerving to a sudden point; the handle surprisingly thin and serious-looking. It would always come in, he supposed.

They drove west for half a day and reached Albi, where they found the strangest cathedral either of them had ever seen: it rose in orange-brown brick, squat yet soaring, church yet fortress, beautiful in spite of being in large parts either ugly or merely odd. The Church militant; also the Church defensive, and the Church symbolic: built as a brick warning to the lingering remnants of Catharism, and to all subsequently tempted by that heresy. As they gazed up at the bulbous, black-faced towers of the west end, at the arrow-slits and the occasional leaping gargoyle, Graham reflected that in a sense this was an oblique, intellectual response to those tumbling heretics of Montaillou: *this* told the dunghill-fornicators that where the strength lay, so did the truth.

Was it her period, or had Graham been a bit edgy for the last couple of days? Even his cheerfulness seemed slightly false. Ann couldn't tell. Maybe it didn't matter; maybe it was just the end of the holiday. In Albi they bought Armagnac and glass jars of vegetables. Graham found some espadrilles and a woven straw hat, both of which he'd been looking for since the start of the trip. They had to use up some of this spare money, he thought; otherwise Ann's walnut box would be overflowing.

As they drove through the outskirts of Toulouse on the way to the airport, they passed a cinema and Ann laughed.

'What's on?' he asked.

'They're showing *Fermeture annuelle*,' she replied. 'It's all over the place.' It was like being on a train in Italy and finding all the towns you went through were called Uscita. 'Is that Godard or Truffaut?'

Graham smiled, and made some appropriate throaty response; but didn't she catch, at the edge of her vision, that instinctive flinch?

At Gatwick they found a taxi without difficulty. It was raining, as it always seemed to be when you returned to England. Graham gazed through the speckled window. Why did everything green seem to have so much brown in it here? And how was it possible for things to be both damp and dusty at the same time? After about a mile, they passed a garage. Four star, three star ... carwash. Graham knew that he was back. The *fermeture annuelle* of the cinema inside his head was over.

# EIGHT

## *The Feminian Sandstones*

Graham felt bad about never taking Alice to the zoo; but there it was. Not that he hated animals: on the contrary, he delighted in their improbability, in the speculative, SF way so many of them had developed. Who played *that* joke on you, he kept wanting to ask them. Whoever thought it was a good idea for you to look like *that*, he whispered to the giraffe. I mean, I know about needing long necks to reach the highest leaves, but wouldn't it have been better-judged to make the trees shorter? Or, for that matter, get used to eating stuff nearer the ground, beetles or scorpions or something? Why did it seem such a good idea to giraffes for them to carry on being giraffes?

Moreover, in a way he would have liked taking Alice round the zoo; it was one place where even the gauchest parent couldn't miss. However cloying, poverty-stricken or contemptible you were in the child's eyes, however frequently you wore the wrong clothes to its school prize day, you could always recoup at the zoo. The animals were so reliably generous with reflected glory—as if they were no more than the momentous products of the parent's imagination. *Look*, my dad invented all these; yes, *and* the crocodile; *and* the emu; *and* the zebra. The only tricky points were sexual: that rhino's erection, hanging down like a flayed gorilla's fist or some joint you don't dare ask for at the butcher's. But even these moments could be explained away in terms of aberrant evolution.

No, the reason Graham dreaded the zoo was because he knew it would make him sad. Shortly after his divorce came through, he'd been discussing visiting rights with Chilton, a cup-of-coffee colleague whose marriage had also broken down.

'Where does she live, your daughter?' Chilton had asked.

'Sort of, well it's hard to describe. In the old days you'd have said Saint Pancras, in the days of the old boroughs, but you know the North London line ... '

Chilton didn't let him finish; not out of irritation, but simply because he already had enough information.

'You'll be able to take her to the zoo then.'

'Oh. Actually I'd been thinking of taking her—well, this Sunday, anyway—up the M1 for tea in a motorway café. Thought that might be something new.'

But Chilton had merely smiled at him knowingly. When, a few weeks later, Ann also implied by a casual remark that she assumed he'd be taking Alice to the zoo that Sunday, Graham hadn't replied, and had carried on reading. Of course, he should have made the connection when Chilton mentioned it. Sunday afternoon was always visiting time: at hospitals, cemeteries, old people's homes, and the houses of separated families. You couldn't take the child back to where you lived because of imagined pollution from some mistress or second wife; you couldn't take it far in the allotted time; and you had to think about tea and lavatories, the two main obsessions of the afternoon child. The zoo was North London's answer: fun, morally okay by the other parent, and stuffed with tea and lavatories.

But Graham didn't want to join in. He imagined the zoo on Sunday afternoons: a few tourists, the occasional keeper, plus sad assemblies of fake-cheerful middle-aged single parents holding on unnecessarily, desperately, to children of various sizes. A time traveller suddenly set down there would conclude that the human race had given up its old method of reproduction, and in his absence had perfected parthenogenesis.

So Graham decided to head off sadness, and never took Alice to the zoo. Once, prompted perhaps by Barbara, his daughter had mentioned its existence, but Graham had taken a firm moral line on the iniquity of keeping animals in captivity. He mentioned battery hens several times, and while his remarks might have sounded pompous to an adult, they struck Alice as high good sense: like most children, she was idealistic and sentimental about Nature, viewing it as something different from Man. Graham, for once, had scored over Barbara with his seemingly principled stand.

Instead, he took Alice to tea-shops and museums and once, unsuccessfully, to a motorway café. There, he failed to allow for her fastidiousness at seeing food for every possible meal lined up democratically behind the counter. The sight of a steak and kidney pudding at four o'clock quite wrecked Alice's chances of appreciating a cupcake.

When it was fine, they walked in parks and looked in the windows of shops that were closed. When it rained, they sometimes just sat in the car and talked.

'Why did you leave Mummy?'

It was the first time she had ever asked, and he didn't know what to say. Instead, he turned the ignition just far enough to start the electrical systems, then switched on the wipers for one clearing sweep. The blur in front of them ceased, and they looked down across a damp park at a pick-up game of football. Within a few seconds the rain had washed the outlines of the players back into hazy patches of colour. Suddenly, Graham felt lost. Why weren't there guides to what you should say? Why wasn't there a consumers' report on broken marriages?

'Because Mummy and I weren't happy together. We weren't ... getting on.'

'You used to tell me you loved Mummy.'

'Yes, well I did. But it sort of stopped.'

'You didn't tell me it stopped. You went on telling me you loved Mummy right up to when you left.'

'Well, I didn't want to ... upset you. You had exams and things.' What things? Her periods?

'I thought you left Mummy for, for her.' The 'her' was neutral, unstressed. Graham knew that his daughter was aware of Ann's name.

'Yes I did.'

'So you didn't leave Mummy because you weren't getting on. You left her because of *her*.' Stressed this time, and not neutral.

'Yes; no; sort of. Mummy and I weren't getting on for a long time before I left.'

'Karen says you ran off because you were feeling middle-aged and wanted to dump Mummy on the scrapheap and swap her for someone younger.'

'No, it wasn't like that.' Who was Karen?

There was a silence. He hoped the conversation was over. He fiddled with the ignition key, but didn't turn it.

'Daddy, was it ... ' Out of the corner of her eye he could see her frown. 'Was it romantic love?' She pronounced it tentatively, as if this was the first time she'd used this foreign phrase.

You couldn't say you didn't know what that meant. You couldn't say, That isn't a real question. There were only two boxes available for answers, and you had to tick one of them quickly.

'Yes, I think you could say it was.'

Saying it—without knowing what it meant, or how the answer would affect Alice—made him feel sadder than if he'd taken her to the zoo.

One, Graham thought. Why was there jealousy—not just for him, but for lots of people? Why did it start up? It was related to love in some way, but that way wasn't quantifiable or comprehensible. Why did it suddenly start wailing in his head, like the ground warning system in an aircraft: six and a half seconds, evasive action, *now*. That was what it felt like sometimes, inside Graham's skull. And why did it pick on him? Was it some bit of fluky chemistry? Was it all dished out at birth? Did you get given jealousy the way you got given a big bottom or poor eyesight, both of which Graham suffered from. If so, maybe it wore off after a while; maybe there was only enough jealousy chemical in that soft box up there for a certain number of years. Perhaps; but Graham rather doubted it: he'd had a big bottom for years, and *that* showed no signs of easing up.

Two. Given that for some reason there had to be jealousy, why should it operate retrospectively? Why was it the only major emotion that seemed to? The others didn't. When he looked at photos of Ann as a girl and a young woman, he felt a natural wish-I'd-been-there wistfulness; and when she told him about some childhood punishment unjustly inflicted on her, he felt protectiveness gurgle up inside him. But these were distanced emotions, felt through gauze; they were easily stirred and easily calmed — calmed by the simple continuance of the present, which wasn't the past. This jealousy, however, came in rushes, in sudden, intimate bursts that winded you; its source was trivial, its cure unknown. Why should the past make you crazy with emotion?

He could think of only one parallel. Some of his students — not many, not even most, but one a year, say — did get incensed about the past. He had a case at present, that ginger-haired boy, MacSomething (God, nowadays it took a whole year to learn their names, and then you never saw them again; you might as well not bother), who became quite enraged by the failure of good (as he saw it) to triumph over evil in History. Why hadn't $x$ prevailed? Why did $z$ beat $y$? He could see MacSomething's puzzled, angry face staring back at him in classes, wanting to be told that History — or at any rate historians — had got it wrong; that $x$ had in fact gone into hiding and turned up years later at $w$; and so on.

Normally, Graham would have ascribed such reactions to — what? — immaturity; or, more specifically, to some local cause like a churchy upbringing. Now he wasn't so sure. MacSomething's rage against the past involved complex emotions about a medley of characters and events. Perhaps he was suffering from a retrospective sense of justice.

Three. Why did retrospective jealousy exist *now*, in the last quarter of the twentieth century? Graham wasn't a historian for nothing. Things died out; rages between nations and continents settled down; civilization *was* becoming more civil: you couldn't deny it, to Graham's eye. Gradually, he didn't doubt, the world would calm down into a gigantic welfare state devoted to sporting, cultural and sexual exchange, with the accepted international currency being items of hifi equipment. There would be the occasional earthquake and volcanic eruption, but even Nature's revenges would be sorted out in time.

So why should this jealousy linger on, unwanted, resented, only there to bugger you around? Like a middle ear, only there to make you lose your sense of balance; or like an appendix, only there to flare up insolently and have to be taken out. How did you take out jealousy?

Four. Why should it happen to him, him of all people? He was, he knew, a very sensible person. Barbara had naturally tried to make him believe that he was a grotesque egomaniac, a monstrous lecher, a heartless emotional dwarf; but that was only understandable. Indeed, the fact that Graham understood it proved to him yet again how sensible he was. Everyone had always called him sensible — his mother comfortingly, his first wife sneeringly, his colleagues applaudingly, his second wife with that fond, mocking, half-askance look in her eye. That's what he was, and he liked being it.

Moreover, it wasn't as if he was one of the world's great lovers. There'd been Barbara, then Ann, and that was more or less all. What he had felt for Barbara had probably been exaggerated by the jaunty novelty of first emotion; while what he felt for Ann, complete as he knew it to be, had arisen warily. And in between? Well, in between, there had been occasions when he'd tried to spur himself into feeling something approaching love; but all he'd ever come up with was a sort of urgent sentimentality.

And since he acknowledged all this about himself, it did seem particularly unfair that he was the one who was being punished. Others kicked the fire but he got burned. Or maybe this was the whole point of it. Maybe this was where Jack's analysis of marriage, Jack's Cross-Eyed Bear, came in. And maybe Jack's theory, correct as far as it went, didn't go far enough. What if it wasn't something in the nature of marriage—in which case, being Jack, you could blame 'society' and then go off and be unfaithful until you felt better about it—but something in the nature of love? That was a much less pleasant thought: that the thing everyone pursued always went wrong, automatically, inevitably, chemically. Graham didn't like the thought of it.

'You could fuck one of your students.'

'No I couldn't.'

'Course you could. Everyone does. That's what they're *for*. I know you're not a looker, but they don't really mind at that age. It's probably more of a turn-on if you're *not* a looker—if you're a bit smelly or fucked-up or depressed. I call it Third World sex. There's a lot of it about, but especially at that age.'

Jack was only trying to be helpful; Graham was practically sure of that.

'Well, I sort of think it's wrong, you see. I mean we are meant to be *in loco parentis*, and it would seem a bit like incest.'

'The family that plays together, stays together.'

Actually, Jack wasn't particularly trying to be helpful. He was a bit fed up with Graham's constant visits. He'd made lots of perfectly good suggestions—that Graham should lie, that he should wank, that he should have a foreign holiday

—and he found that his therapist's bag was more or less empty. In any case, he'd only felt half-sorry for Graham in the first place. Now, he felt almost more inclined to fool around with his friend than indulge him.

'... and in any case,' Graham was continuing, 'I don't want to.'

'Appetite comes with eating.' Jack cocked an eyebrow, but Graham stolidly took the remark as no more than a platitude.

'The funny thing is—I mean, the thing that's most surprised me about it all—is that it's so visual.'

' ... ?'

'Well, I've always been a words man myself. I would be, wouldn't I? It's always been words that have most affected me. I don't like pictures much; I'm not interested in colours or clothes; I don't even like pictures in books; and I hate films. Well, I used to hate films. Well, I still do, though in a different way, of course.'

'Yes.' Jack waited for Graham to come to the point. This, he realized, was why he preferred sane people to crazy people: crazy people took so long to come to the point; they thought you wanted a Red Rover tour of their psyche before they showed you Buckingham Palace. They thought that everything was interesting, that everything was relevant. Jack tried to think up a new joke. Could he do anything with Edgar Wind? Or what about a wind quintet? No, that would be straining the old sphincter a bit. And they didn't seem to have wind duos.

'But it was a surprise that the visual thing really triggered it off ... '

Wasn't there a River Windrush somewhere? Hmmm, might take a bit of planning.

' ... I mean, obviously I *knew* when Ann and I married that it wasn't like when Barbara and I married. And of course Ann was always completely straightforward with me about chaps ... about her life ... before she met me ... '

Do it as you tripped up and you could have a *windfall*. Maybe an apple as prop? Down at the coast and you could have Come wind or high water; maybe use that with the washing-up?

' … so I knew some of their names, and I might even have seen a photo or two, though of course I didn't look hard; and I knew what jobs they'd done, and some were younger than me of course and some were better-looking and some were richer and some were probably better in bed, but it was all right. It was … '

Windhover. Windlass. Windjammer. Jack suppressed a half-chuckle, and politely turned it into a grunt.

' … it really was. And then I went to see *Over the Moon* and it all changed. Now why should I, who have been untouched by the visual for my whole life, suddenly go under like that? I mean, haven't you thought about it yourself—it must affect you, professionally, I mean, if some people get more out of films than books.'

'I always say you can take a book anywhere. Can't see a film on the can, can you?'

'No, that's true. But seeing my wife there, up there on the screen, it was all quite different. I mean the visual— the visual is just a lot more powerful than the word, isn't it?'

'I think your case is a bit special.'

'Maybe it's the public thing as well—thinking of other people seeing her up there. A sort of public cuckolding.'

'Her films weren't like *that*, were they? And I wouldn't think many of the audience were nudging one another and saying, Hey, isn't that Graham's missus? As she wasn't at that time anyway.'

'No, true.' Maybe the public thing wasn't the case. But the visual thing was. He lapsed into silence. Jack continued peacefully with his inward dictionary-flipping. After a bit Graham said,

'What are you thinking?'

Ah, shit; he was actually working on *windbag*. Better improvise.

'Nothing much, to be honest  Nothing helpful. I was just wondering what "Feminian" means.'

' ... ?'

'I wonder if it's a real geological term, or if Kipling just made it up. It sounds so close to "feminine" that I suppose it must be real, but I've never found it in a dictionary. Or maybe he did make it up, but miscalculated a bit.'

' ... ?'

'On the first Feminian sandstones we were promised the
Fuller Life
(Which started by loving our neighbour and ended by loving
his wife).'

If that doesn't make him go, Jack thought, nothing will. But instead Graham replied,

'Do you know what I discovered the French for?'

' ... '

'You ever seen a bull's balls?'

'Mmm.' Which didn't mean Yes or No, but Get on with it.

'Huge, aren't they? And all long, you could almost play rugger with them, couldn't you?'

' ... '

'We were passing a butcher's in France — in Castres — and saw some in the window. I mean, they must have been bull's, I can't think of anything that size, unless they were horse's, but this wasn't a horse-butcher's, so I suppose that rules out ... '

' ... '

'And I said to Ann, Let's go in and ask what they are, and she giggled a bit and said, Well, it's obvious what they are, isn't it, and I said, Yes we know what they *are* but let's find out what they're *called*, and we went in and there was this very precise French butcher, very finickity, looked as if he knew how to cut meat without making it bleed, and Ann

127

said to him, "Can you tell us what those are," pointing at the tray, and you know what he said?'

' ... '

'He said, "*Ce sont des frivolités, Madame.*" Isn't that good?'

'Not bad.'

'And then we thanked him and walked out.'

' ... ' (I didn't think you bought them for sandwiches, for Christ's sake.)

'*Frivolités.*' Graham murmured the word again and nodded to himself, like an old man suddenly warmed by the thought of a picnic forty years ago. Jack stirred himself to a final comment.

'Actually, there's a bloke in America with no past, you know.'

'Nnn?'

'Really. I read about it. Seems he was fencing, and his opponent's foil went right up his nose and into his brain. Destroyed his memory. He's been like that for twenty years.'

'Amnesia,' said Graham, peeved by this irrelevance.

'No, not really. It's better than that. Or worse, I suppose —I mean, the piece I read didn't say whether the bloke was happy or not. But the point is, he can't form any new memories either. Forgets everything straight away. Think of that—no archives at all. Maybe you'd like that?'

' ... '

'Wouldn't you? No archives—just the present? Like staring out of a train window all the time. The cornfield, the telegraph poles, the washing lines, the tunnel: no connections, no causation, no sense of repetition.'

' ... '

'They could probably do it for you. Fork up the sniffer and bob's your auntie. I expect you can get it on the National Health by now.'

Graham sometimes wondered if Jack was taking him seriously.

For several weeks after they returned from France things held together. Ann found herself watching Graham in a way she half-recognized without ever having experienced before. She was watching him as you might watch an alcoholic or a potential suicide, tacitly giving him marks for performing quite ordinary actions, like eating his breakfast cereal, and changing gear, and not falling through the television screen. Of course, she was sure he wasn't either of those things—an alcoholic or a potential suicide. It was true he drank a bit more than he used to; and it was also true that Jack, in his own tactful way, had hinted to her that Graham was completely off his head. But Ann knew better. She knew her husband better for a start; and she also knew Jack. He always preferred life to be lurid and people to be crackers, because that made things more interesting. It somehow seemed to justify his vocation.

After the curse went away, Ann waited for Graham to want to make love to her; but he didn't seem very keen. She would generally go to bed first; he would make some excuse and stay downstairs. When he did come to bed he would kiss her on the forehead and then get into his sleeping position almost at once. Ann minded, but also didn't mind: she'd rather he didn't if he didn't want to; the fact that he didn't try faking it meant, she supposed, that there was still an honest bond between them.

Often he slept badly, kicking out clumsily in his dreams at imaginary opponents, mumbling and making sharp squeaks like a panicking rodent. He fought with his bedclothes and she would find, on getting up before him, that his side of the bed had come completely untucked.

On one such morning she went round and looked at him as he lay on his back asleep and half-exposed. His face was calm, but both his hands were raised beside his head, their palms open and upturned. Her eye travelled down his academic chest with its erratic growth of mousy hair, and on over the thickening waist to the genitals. His cock, smaller and seemingly pinker than usual, lay at right angles across his left thigh; one of his balls was trapped out of sight; the other, its chicken-skin pulled tight, lay close up underneath his cock. Ann gazed at the moonscape of this ball, at the fissured, bumpy skin, the surprising hairlessness. How puzzling that so much trouble could be caused by so trifling, so odd-looking an organ. Maybe one should just ignore it; maybe it didn't matter. Looked at in the morning light, while its proprietor lay sleeping, the whole pink-brown outfit struck Ann as strangely unimportant. After a while, it didn't even look as if it had anything much to do with sex. Yes, that was right: what was nestling at the join of Graham's thigh wasn't anything to do with sex at all — it was just a peeled prawn and a walnut.

The butcher wore a blue-striped apron and a straw hat with a blue ribbon round it. For the first time in years, waiting in the queue, Ann thought what a strange contrast the apron and the hat made. The boater implied the idle splash of an oar in a listless, weed-choked river; the blood-stained apron announced a life of crime, of psychopathic killing. Why had she never noticed that before? Looking at this man was like looking at a schizophrenic: civility and brutishness hustled together into a pretence of normality. And people *did* think it was normal; they weren't astonished that this man, just by standing there, could be announcing two incompatible things.

'Yes, my lovely?'

She had almost forgotten what she'd come for.

'Two pork fillets, please, Mr Walker.'

The butcher slapped them like fish on to his broad scale.

'Half a dozen eggs. Large brown. No, may as well make it a dozen.'

Walker, with his back to Ann, raised an eyebrow quietly to himself.

'And could I order a Chateaubriand for Saturday?'

As the butcher turned round again he gave her a smile.

'Thought you'd tire of the old tripe and onions after a while.'

Ann laughed; as she left the shop she thought, What funny things tradesmen say; I suppose it's part of the patter; all customers must look alike after a while; and my hair *is* dirty. The butcher meanwhile was thinking, Well, I'm glad *he*'s got his job back; or a new one; or whatever.

Ann told Graham about the butcher mistaking her for someone else, but he only grunted in reply. All right, she thought, it's not *that* interesting, but it's something to say. Graham was getting more silent and withdrawn. She seemed to do all the talking nowadays. Which was why she found herself bringing up things like the butcher. And when she did, he grunted, as if to say, the *reason* I'm not as talkative as you expect me to be is because you mention such boring things. Once she had been in the middle of trying to describe a new fabric she had seen at work when he suddenly looked up and said,

'Don't care.'

'Don't Care was made to care,' she answered instinctively. It was what her grandmother had always replied when, as a child, Ann expressed pert indifference. And if her 'Don't care' had implied genuine recalcitrance, her grandmother used to give the full reply:

> Don't Care was made to care;
> Don't Care was hung;
> Don't Care was put in a pot
> And boiled till she was done.

There were still three weeks of Graham's summer holiday left (Ann could never get used to calling it 'vacation'). Normally, this was one of the best times of the year, when Graham was at his most helpful and jolly. She would go to work happy at the thought of him messing about at home, reading a bit, sometimes making the dinner. Occasionally, in the last year or two, she had sneaked off work in the middle of the afternoon, getting back sweaty and sexy from the heat and the light clothes she wore and the thump and rattle of the Underground; without speaking they'd agree on why she'd come home early, and they would go to bed with her still damp at all the hinges of her body.

Afternoon sex was the best sex of all, Ann thought. Morning sex she'd had enough of in her time: usually it meant, 'Sorry about last night but here it is anyway'; and sometimes it meant, '*This*'ll make sure you don't forget me today'; but neither attitude charmed her. Evening sex was, well, your basic sex, wasn't it? It was the sex which could vary from enveloping happiness via sleepily given consent to an edgy, 'Look, this is what we came to bed early *for*, so why don't we just get on with it.' Evening sex was as good or as indifferent, and certainly as unpredictable, as sex could be. But afternoon sex – that was never just a courteous way to round things off; it was keen, intended sex. And sometimes it whispered to you, in a curious way (and even though you were married), 'This is what we're doing now, and I still want to spend the evening with you afterwards.' Afternoon sex gave you unexpected comforts like that.

Once Ann had tried for it since they got back from France. But when she got home, Graham wasn't there, even though he'd said he'd be in all day. She felt parched and disappointed, and walked round petulantly checking the rooms. She made herself a cup of coffee. As she sipped it, she freewheeled slowly down to disappointment and beyond. They couldn't make love; he'd just buggered off; whereas if he had any instinct, any nous ... She grumbled to herself at men's structural inability to catch moods, to seize the day. Then she paused: perhaps he had gone out intending to come back in time. What if something had happened? How long does it take you to find out? Who rings you? Within fifteen seconds she had arrived at the predictive pleasure of widowhood. Go on, then, die, don't come back, see if I care.

In quick succession she saw a bus stalled across the road, a pair of crushed spectacles, an ambulance man's shroud.

Then she remembered Margie, a schoolfriend who'd fallen, in her mid-twenties, for a married man. He'd left his family, set up house with her, moved in all his things, and got a divorce. They talked about having children. Two months later he was dead of a perfectly normal, extremely rare blood disease. Years afterwards Margie had confessed to Ann her feelings. 'I loved him very much. I planned to spend the rest of my life with him. I'd messed up his family so even if I hadn't wanted to see it through I would have. Then he got thin and white and drained away from me, and I watched him die. And the day after he died, I found something inside me saying, "You're free." Over and over again, "You're free." Even though I didn't want to be.'

Ann hadn't understood, not until this moment. She wanted Graham home *now*, safe; she also wanted him under a bus, stretched and burned across a tube line, impaled on the driving shaft of the car. The two wishes coexisted; they didn't even begin to war.

By the time Graham got home, at about seven, her feelings had subsided. He claimed he'd suddenly remembered something he wanted to look up in the library. She didn't think about whether or not she believed him, never asked any more if he'd seen any good films lately. He didn't seem to think there was anything to apologize for. He was a little subdued, and went off to take a bath.

Graham was more or less telling the truth. In the morning, after Ann had left, he'd finished the paper and done the washing up. Then he wandered round the house like a burglar, finding each room a surprise. He had ended up, as always, in his study. He *could* start that new biography of Balfour, which he'd even gone as far as buying. He quite wanted to, because nowadays biographies, or so it seemed to him, were more and more about sex. Historians, lethargic buggers at the best of times, had finally arrived at a filtered awareness of Freud. Suddenly, it all boiled down to sex. Did Balfour deliver the goods? Was Hitler monorchid? Was Stalin a Great Terror in bed? As a research method, it had as much chance, Graham judged, of turning up the truth as did wading through boxes of state papers.

He quite wanted to learn about Balfour's frigidity; and in a sense he needed to, as a few of his more assiduous students might be speed-reading the book at this very moment. But in a larger sense he didn't. After all, he wasn't going to switch his approach to the study of history from intuitive-pragmatic (as he currently thought of it) to psycho-sexual; it would stir up the department too much for a start. And besides, even if every single student next term had read this biography (which seemed to get fatter and fatter in his mind the longer he left it unread), he, Graham, would still know far more about everything than all of them put together. Most of them didn't know much when they started, got bored early on, read just enough to get by, borrowed each other's notes for the exams, and were happy to get any sort of degree. You only had to toss the name of an authority at them for them all to look scared. Is it long, their expressions asked, and, Can I get by without it? Graham tended to throw in a number of discouraging names during the first few weeks; but mainly he relied on a system of boring them. *Pas trop d'enthousiasme.* Don't over-excite them, he'd say to himself as he faced his first-year classes; you never know what you might be letting yourself in for.

So instead of Balfour he fished in the 1915–19 drawer of his filing cabinet. There was one girl in the new magazine he was really looking forward to wanking with. Most of the girls in most of the magazines, of course, were good for a heavy flirtation, even—if your fingers misled you at a vital juncture—for a consummation. But somehow every magazine always yielded up a favourite, someone to come back to, someone to think of with fondness, to half look out for in the street.

'Brandy' was his current favourite; a soft-faced, almost bookish girl. Indeed, in one shot she was pictured reading a hardback; probably something from a book club, he thought disapprovingly, but even so, better than nothing. And the contrast between this gentle face and the vigorous, almost aggressive way she turned out her trouser pocket struck Graham with piercing force, time after time. 'Brandy makes you randy' announced the corny letterpress; but it was quite true.

In the bathroom, Graham re-read the whole magazine except for the pages devoted to Brandy (why wasn't she the centre-fold, he demanded angrily: *much* better than whatser-name in that *Tom Jones* sequence, all embroidered cami-knickers and *soft focus* for Christ's sake). Whereas Brandy, revealed in fearsome detail towards the back of the maga-zine ... Just a couple more pages of readers' letters and the massage parlour ads, and you can turn to her, he promised himself. Okay, right, now. His left hand found Brandy while his right hand became more serious. Check again how many pages there are of her, yes eight, that's three double spreads and one at the start and one at the end, best double spread on pages six and seven, okay, start at the end, Christ yes, she is, isn't she, then back to the beginning, and one, yes, then over and mmmmm, then yes *that* shot, and now, over, and time to look at each of the three pictures slowly, lovingly, before *that one, that one*. Perfect.

After lunch he settled down in front of the television and tuned in to I.T.V.; he switched on the V.C.R., pressed the Record button, and then immediately the Pause. That way he wouldn't lose two or three vital seconds. He sat there for over an hour watching genre serials before seeing what he wanted and flipping up the Pause. Fifteen seconds later he pressed the Stop button. Then he replayed the whole tape. It didn't bother him at first; but later he began to brood. Maybe he should drive up to Colindale; that might keep sadness at bay. It was strange how violent sadness could be.

It was strange, too, how it was possible to be both entirely happy and entirely sad. Perhaps you were compelled to be this sad if you had been this happy. Perhaps the two were linked, like the weathermen on a cuckoo clock. Cuckoo, he thought, cuckoo. Which one of you is coming out next?

Jack had an insincere way of smiling as well as a sincere one. This was a discovery it took Sue some years to make; but the distinction, once spotted, was an unfailing indicator of behaviour. The insincere smile involved showing rather more of the upper teeth, and was held for slightly longer than necessary; there were doubtless other subtleties, but these were lost beneath the beard.

Most weekends Jack had been voluble about the Hendricks, and keen to speculate even if there had been no new developments. Sue looked forward to the latest episode in their friends' soap opera. She wasn't fond enough of them to be apprehensive. But this Friday her enquiry received the grunted reply,

'No couchwork this week.'

'What do you think they're up to?'

'Dunno.'

'Come on. Guess.' He obviously needed coaxing; perhaps she'd come back to it tomorrow. But she realized she wouldn't when he looked across at her, showed more of his teeth than normal, and answered,

'I think the subject's run out of steam, my dovey.'

Every time she saw that smile Sue felt she knew what it must be like to hate Jack. Not that she did — and besides, Jack always worked hard at making himself liked — but whenever he smiled like that she thought to herself, 'Yes, of course; and what's more, it would feel like that *all the time*.' Because the first such smile had accompanied her first discovery that Jack had been unfaithful to her. It marked the end of what she termed her Tully River Blacks phase.

At the time it happened Sue had recently read an article about the Tully River Blacks, a small tribe of Australian aboriginals, reputedly the only people in the world who had not yet grasped the link between sex and conception. They thought sex was something you did for fun, like daubing yourself with mud or whatever, and that conception was a gift from heaven which arrived mysteriously—though it might be affected by the way you threw the bones or gutted the wallaby. It was surprising, really, that there weren't more tribes around like this.

There was another theory about the Tully River Blacks, of course. This was that they knew very well which cause had which effect, and were seeing how long they could bamboozle the teams of patronizing anthropologists who got so excited about their wry fable. They'd only invented it in the first place because they were fed up with being asked about the Great Hunter in the sky; and anyway, like most people, they preferred to talk about fucking than about God. But their lie had a marvellous effect, and had kept the tribe in chocolate and transistor radios ever since.

Sue guessed which of the two interpretations Jack would favour; but then men were more cynical than women. Women believed until there was overwhelming evidence not to. Which was what her Tully River Blacks phase was all about. It had ended ten months after they were married, though the dossier available to her by then ought to have proved more than sufficient. Over a period of five weeks there had been the Lost Shirt, the Sudden Interest in Buying Toothpaste, the Cancelled Last Train from Manchester, and the Playful Scuffle over her not being allowed to read one of Jack's 'fan' letters. But none of it meant anything until Jack showed her his upper teeth and held on to that smile for a second too long; whereupon all the bits cascaded into place and she knew he'd been fucking someone else. Her only mild, distant consolation was that the Tully River Blacks, if they *were* naive, would probably feel a whole lot sicker than she did when the anthropologists finally decided to fill them in on The Connection.

She taught herself early on not to pursue the false smile. Never ask. It hurt less, and then you forgot until the next time. So she didn't bother to follow up Jack's last dissuasive remark about the Hendricks; to ask, for instance, whether his couch had been used for more practical therapeutic purposes.

The answer would have been No, though its circumstances probably wouldn't have comforted her. Jack had made a bit of a pass at Ann that week. Well, she kept turning up, didn't she, and often on what seemed to him little enough pretext. He knew their affair had been officially shredded. But as against that, she did keep turning up, and what with Graham wanking away like a cotton mill ... It wasn't really his fault, he thought; it was just the nature of the beast. If I wasn't unfaithful, he quoted, I wouldn't be true to myself.

So he had tried. Well, sometimes it was the only courteous thing to do, wasn't it? And Ann was an old friend: she wouldn't take it the wrong way. What's more, he hadn't exactly frightened the horses. Just got hold of her as she was leaving, kissed her more accurately than mere friendship demanded, drawn her away from the front door and gently led her to the foot of the stairs. And the funny thing was, she'd allowed herself to be led that far. She'd walked half a dozen yards or so with his arm round her before breaking away in a silent flurry and heading for the door. She hadn't yelped, or hit him, or even seemed hugely surprised. So really, he was thinking, as he looked across at Sue and gave her a winning smile, he'd been a perfectly faithful husband. What grounds had anyone for complaint?

Graham's holiday photos didn't come out, which only half-surprised him. Occasionally, when he had wound on, he'd felt the ridged knob transfer to his thumb suspicions of the camera's inner turbulence; but as long as the knob still turned, he hoped for the best. The processors printed the first eight shots—Ann sitting on a farmhouse with a goat tethered to her leg; the other half of the farmhouse wittily nestling in the ramparts at Carcassonne—but then gave up.

Despite Ann's suggestions that they were all funny, and some of them even quite arty, Graham just grunted and threw them away. He also threw away the negatives. Later, he regretted this. He found it surprisingly hard to remember the holiday, even after five weeks. He remembered that he had been happy on it; but without the visual corroboration of where he had been happy, the memory of that emotion seemed valueless. Even a blurry double image would have been something.

Why should this happen: this, on top of Ann's films and his magazines? Up in his brain, had a set of points suddenly been switched to make him visually responsive? But could that happen after forty-odd years—forty-odd years of being a words man? At some stage, obviously, the whole soft box just began to wear out; bits fell off it; muscles—if they had such things there—got tired and stopped functioning properly. He could ask his friend Bailey, the gerontologist, about that. But at fortyish? What could account for such a shift in perceptions? You thought about your brain, when you did, as something you used—put things into and got out answers. Now, suddenly, you felt as if it were using you: sitting up there with a life of its own, and giving the rudder a tweak just at the point when you thought everything was going sweetly. What if your brain became your enemy?

# NINE

# *Sometimes a Cigar ...*

It was Ann who suggested they gave a party. For one thing, it might make the place feel less like a police station; and it would, however briefly, break the depressing routine of their evenings. At the moment, after a dinnertime of proxy complaints and defiant drinking, Graham would retreat silently to his study; Ann would sit reading, watching television, but mainly waiting for Graham to come downstairs. She felt as if she were sitting in a moulded plastic chair in front of a metal desk, breathing an atmosphere of stale cigarettes and waiting for the two of them to come through the door: the gentle one who only wanted to help you, and the anarchically brutal one who could freeze you by merely flicking your shoulder blade.

After an hour or so Graham would come downstairs and go into the kitchen. She would hear the clatter of ice into a glass; or, sometimes, two glasses. If it was two glasses, he'd be in a benign mood: that's to say, benignly depressed. He'd hand her a drink and murmur:

> 'Between the study and the bed
> Liquor stands me in good stead.'

Then he'd sit down beside her and either join in a bad television programme, or maunder on about how he loved her, or both. She hated being told like this that she was loved; it sounded like one extra thing to feel guilty about.

More frequently, though, it was the other one who came

downstairs: the one with a single drink in his hand. He knew precisely what your crime was, and didn't wait to hear it from you, but went ahead and read the charges as if they were verdicts. And when Graham was in this mood—which was about two nights out of three—he would rail at her, repeating strings of names and recounting his horrible dreams: dreams of adultery, mutilation and revenge. At times she wondered if they had really happened, if they weren't just inventions made up to appal her.

And always, even on the most brutal evenings, he would crack: after an hour, an hour and a half, when she'd fetched herself a drink to keep going, when he'd fetched himself several more, when he'd interrogated her about the most improbable liaisons, he'd suddenly fall silent, and then begin to weep. His head would droop, and the tears which invaded his eyes would fill up his lenses, then suddenly burst out, down both sides of his nose as well as his cheeks. He cried in four streams instead of the usual two, and it looked twice as sad. Afterwards, Graham would tell her that all his incomprehensible anger was directed, not at her, but at himself; that he had nothing to reproach her for, and that he loved her.

Ann knew he was telling the truth, and also knew she would never abandon him. Leaving him wouldn't solve anything. Besides, they both believed he was quite sane. Jack's casual suggestion to Ann that a shrink might help was scarcely discussed. You had to be either more arrogant or more insecure to do that, she thought. You had to be less ordinary, less English. This was just one of those hiccups all marriages go through. A severe hiccup, it was true—more like whooping-cough—but both Graham and Ann believed that he would come through in the end. Still, it was a lonely process; even Jack had seemed less keen on giving up his time lately—especially after she had turned away from the foot of his stairs.

And so, most nights, Ann would sit quietly through

Graham's outbursts, and at the end of the evening would stroke the side of his head and dry his tears with a handkerchief. Then she would lead him up to bed, and they would lie there, exhausted by sadness. On their backs, side by side, they looked like figures on a tomb.

Ann screened the guests with some care. No old boyfriends, naturally. Jack would have to come, but that was all right — history had been rewritten. No one who knew too much about her past; and no one, she decided, who might want to flirt with her after a few drinks. It was beginning to sound like a soya meal.

'What shall we say it's for?' Graham wondered over lunch.

'We don't have to, do we?'

'We might be asked. Parties are always *for* something, aren't they?'

'Don't people give parties just for the sake of giving parties?'

'Can't we do better than that?'

'Well, it can be our wedding anniversary or something.'

After lunch, as she carried on clearing up the house — which meant, she realized, emptying it of its keenest references to the people who lived there, making it as much a public place as possible — Ann found herself pondering more precisely what it was for. Perhaps, she concluded, it was a sort of announcement to their friends that nothing was wrong. The fact that none of their friends, apart from Jack, knew or suspected that anything was wrong in the first place was neither here nor there.

The first person Ann opened the door to was Jack.

'Point me at the pussy. Oops. Oh God, fled already, has it?'

'You're early, Jack. Graham isn't even ready yet.'

'Shit, so I am. Bought this digital watch, you see. Couldn't understand the twenty-four hour system. Only took off ten. Started standing people up by two hours. Now I'm over-compensating. Take off fourteen instead.' Jack put on a that-sounds-unconvincing expression. He looked and sounded nervous. 'Actually, I thought I'd come and see everything was all right. What's it about anyway?'

'Oh, wedding anniversary.'

'Bloody good.'

'Yes.'

'Mmmm, but it wasn't, was it?'

' ... ?'

'I mean, I was there.'

'Christ, Jack—the first person I try it on ... sorry, love.'

'More rewriting history, eh?'

'Well ... '

'Don't worry, I won't blab. What's the crumpet factor?'

'Don't you ever ease up, Jack?'

'Always trying to ease up. Ease up who's the question.'

'Maybe you should be a bit discreet this evening.'

'Ah, catch the drift. Still, have to seem natural, don't I?'

'You could start by opening some wine.'

'Roger, wilco, *sah*.' Jack seemed very ill at ease for once. Normally, you could rely on him to be himself. His ebullience might fluctuate, but he was always reliably self-obsessed. That was why he was so useful socially. He made other people feel at ease by knowing they didn't have to talk about themselves unless they really wanted to.

Jack's way of opening wine was manly and combative. He wouldn't use openers which relied on air-injection systems; he called them chicks' bicycle-pumps. He wouldn't use wooden contraptions which fitted over the neck of the bottle and offered a choice of handles to turn. He would not even use a simple waiter's corkscrew: the idea of a lever and a two-pull technique struck him as cissy. All he would contemplate was a simple, old-fashioned, wooden-handled corkscrew.

The performance was a three-part ritual. One: corkscrew inserted at waist height on a table or sideboard. Two: bottle picked up, held only by the corkscrew, and lowered in a smooth swoop to a position between the feet. Three: feet clamped round the base of the bottle, left hand holding the neck, then the cork pulled in a long, single stroke as if starting a motor mower; as the right arm came up with its prize, so, in parallel but belated motion, the left arm came up with the bottle, which was smoothly returned to its original surface. The performance, Jack believed, was one in which natural strength was subdued into elegant line.

He opened the first six bottles by himself, in the kitchen. Graham walked in as he was removing the foil from the neck of the seventh. His trick with foil was to take it off in one long strip, like apple peel.

'Just in time,' he bellowed at Graham, and went straight into his three-part act. As he drew the cork, the natural pop was followed by what Graham thought at first might be an echo. But Jack was smiling to himself and gazing at the wine; he muttered,

'It's an ill wind ... '

Graham wondered if he ever farted for women. You couldn't very well ask. You couldn't ask the women, because you couldn't; and you couldn't ask Jack because it was too late now, because the joke for him, and whatever there was of it for you, somehow depended on its inwardness, on its being not heard but overheard. The nearest you came to acknowledgment was to murmur, as Graham did now,

'Bless you.'

Jack smiled again; he was beginning to feel more at ease.

Nobody arrived for twenty minutes, and the three of them sat in the sitting-room while it swelled to the size of a hangar; then, as if suddenly released from a traffic-jam, half the guests came together. There were coats to be laid tenderly on beds, and drinks to get, and introductions to make while the guests' eyes searched anxiously for ashtrays and ashtray lookalikes. And after half an hour the party began to run itself; people started to treat the hosts as guests, filling their glasses and offering to fetch them food.

Ann enlisted Jack's help in forcing the guests to mix; Graham pottered around with a wine bottle in one hand and a glass of whisky in the other; and the noise level rose in its usual baffling way—not because more people had arrived, but in a self-willed, uncontrollable spiral.

Jack, of course, was normally at the head of these sound spirals. He was standing about eight feet away, engaging the attention of two of the plainest models Ann had been able to lay her hands on: chunky girls who specialized in showing county tweeds and trench-coats. But all models are chameleons, and somehow they had managed to make themselves look slim and debby. Jack, in mid-act, caught Ann's eye on him and winked. One of the debby girls turned; Ann nodded and smiled, but didn't come across.

Jack was smoking a cigar. 'Have a nun's dildo,' he would normally chortle, taking out a pack of panatellas. Ann doubted if he'd used that line yet, though he had always assured her that the posher the girl, the dirtier you should talk. It was interesting—and well-judged—that he was smoking a cigar. The cigarette trick, he must have decided, was not the right approach for these girls; something more autocratic was called for. And the funny thing was, Jack looked just as plausible with a cigar as he did with a cigarette. His image readjusted itself without any difficulty.

Ann's refill route gradually took her nearer Jack and the two models. As she approached she heard him preparing for one of his favourite lines.

' … but a good cigar is a smoke. Still, that's only Kipling. Do you like Kipling? Don't know, never been kippled; I understand. No, the thing about cigars and women, Kipling got it all wrong, didn't he?' (the questions were always rhetorical) 'the thing about *that* is, really, well, Freud, isn't it?'

The models looked at one another.

'You know what Freud said on the subject?'

They didn't. Freud meant a few basic things to them:

145

snakes, and everything being really about sex, and other things they didn't want to think about: things about your bottom, they suspected. They giggled a little in anticipation, and waited on Jack. He rocked on his heels, put a thumb in the pocket of his leather waistcoat, waggled his cigar suggestively up and down, then took a long, roguish puff.

'Freud said,' and he paused again, ' "Sometimes a cigar … is only a cigar." '

The models whinnied in a mixture of amusement and relief, pushing the noise spiral still higher. Ann moved across to join them, and Jack patted her welcomingly on the bottom.

'Welcome, my lovely,' he roared, though he was standing right next to her; indeed his arm was now round her shoulder. Ann turned her head towards him and made to whisper. He felt the turn through his arm, caught the head-movement from the corner of his eye, deduced that he was being offered a kiss, and twisted into it with a horizontal swoop. Ann succeeded at the last moment in avoiding his lips, but still received a severe graze of cigar-fumed beard across her cheek.

'Jack,' she whispered, 'I think the arm is a bad idea.' The models, while unable to hear her request, noticed how quickly Jack dropped his arm; it was almost a parody of parade-ground smartness.

'Thing about Freud is … ' Ann smiled her departure. Jack was going into one of his prepared speeches about how Freud's interpretations of dreams were either obvious ('Woman walks up Krautstrasse, buys herself a black hat; the old buffoon charges her 5,000 krone to tell her she wants her husband to be dead') or unverifiably fantastic; how the cure rate for those who went to shrinks was no higher than for those who went on being crackers by themselves; how, in terms of the science of understanding people, the novelist's methods were much older and more sophisticated; how anyone who wanted to lie down on *his* couch for an hour or two and give him free material was welcome; how they could play whatever role, or whatever game, they liked; how *his* favourite game (a puckish wink would be thrown in here) was Strip Jack Naked ...

Ann refilled some glasses, stirred up a stagnant area in the corner of the room, and looked around for Graham. She couldn't see him in the sitting-room, so went through into the kitchen. There was a tramp raiding the refrigerator. At second glance, it was only Bailey, the gerontologist colleague of Graham's, who, despite private wealth, always tried to look as shabby as possible, and usually succeeded. He kept his raincoat on, even in the house; his lank hair might have been whitish if it hadn't been filthy.

'Thought I might fry up some offal,' he said, with a property-is-theft glance into the fridge.

'Make yourself at home,' said Ann superfluously. 'Seen Graham?'

Bailey merely shook his head and carried on unwrapping polythene bags.

Probably having a pee. She gave him a couple of minutes; then another couple, in case there was a queue. Then she went up to his study, knocked gently, and turned the knob. The room was dark. She went inside, and waited until her eyes adjusted themselves. No, he wasn't hiding. Casually, she looked down into the garden, the nearer part of which was lit from the sitting-room's french windows. At the bottom end, in the darkest part, Graham was sitting on the rockery, staring back towards the house.

She went quickly downstairs and drew the sitting-room curtains. Then she returned to the kitchen, where Bailey, fork in hand, was spearing half-cooked pieces of chicken liver out of the frying pan. She seized a plate, tipped the contents of the pan on to it, thrust it into his hand, and pushed the pseudo-derelict towards the sitting-room. 'Circulate, Mr Bailey,' she demanded.

Then she walked through the kitchen and out of the side door. When she reached Graham he was sitting on a large

147

stone, his left shoe crushing some aubretia; clamped between his feet was a half-empty bottle of Haig. He was frowning vaguely towards the now-curtained french windows. From here, the peaks and troughs of party noise were flattened into a steady medium band of sound.

Ann felt sorry for Graham, and also more irritated than ever before. The conflict resolved itself into a middle, professional tone.

'Graham, is anything the matter? Or are you just drunk?'

He avoided her eye, and didn't reply immediately. Sometimes, he felt, this was all life consisted of: wives asking you aggrieved questions. Fifteen years of it with Barbara. When he met Ann, he thought all that was over. Now it seemed to be starting up again. Why couldn't he be left in peace?

'Drunk yes,' he finally said. '*Just* drunk no. Matter.'

'What is the matter?'

'Ah. Matter. Matter is seeing wife kissing friend. Matter matter. Seeing best friend stroking wife's ... behind. Matter matter.'

So that was it. Where had he been standing? But in any case, why the hell shouldn't she let Jack Lupton kiss her at a party? With difficulty she maintained her nurse-like tone.

'Graham, I kissed Jack because I was pleased to see him and he'd been doing his best to make the party go well, which is more than I can say for you at the moment. He put his arm round me because, because he's Jack. I left him with Deanna and Joanie, and he was doing very well for himself.'

'Ah. Sorry. Sorry. My fault. Didn't help at party enough. Jack helps. Jack gets to pat wife's bottom for helping. Must be more helpful. Good old Jack, jolly old Jack. Matter?' he addressed the Haig bottle, 'No matter. Matter gone away. Wife kisses helper. Matter gone. All gone.'

Ann wasn't sure she could keep her temper. She picked up the Haig and walked back towards the house, emptying it over the lawn as she went. She closed the back door and locked it. She reappeared in the sitting-room with a bottle of wine in each hand, by way of explaining her absence. She mentioned here and there that Graham had overdone the drink and was sleeping it off upstairs. The news spread gradually, and with a few muted smiles people began to leave. Jack, having made a late push to separate Deanna and Joanie, left with both of them.

There were only three guests remaining when Graham attacked the french window with a garden fork. The tines slipped at first and glanced off the pane, so he reversed his hold and smashed the glass with the handle. Then he methodically chipped away the loose shards until there was a hole large enough for him to stoop through. He threw the fork up the lawn like a javelin—it stuck, held, swivelled, and flopped flat—then, pushing the curtain ahead of him, climbed back into his house. As he disentangled himself and blinked at the light, he saw in front of him his wife, his colleague Bailey, and a young couple whom he couldn't remember meeting. The man had a bottle aloft in expectation of a crazed burglar. It was a full bottle.

'Careful. Two twenty-five, that stuff. Use the white if you have to.' Then he walked unsteadily to an armchair and sat down. It occurred to him that he probably ought to explain his behaviour. 'Ah,' he said. 'Locked out. Sorry. Sorry. Didn't have my key.'

Ann shepherded the guests to the front door. Overwork. Worried about the party. Too much to drink. Daughter not been well (she invented that). On the pavement Bailey turned, looked very carefully at her, and announced, as if it were an episcopal blessing,

'Never mix, never worry.'

'That's a wise thought, Mr Bailey. I'll pass it on.'

She went back inside, fetched some Sellotape and newspapers, and patched over the window. Then she poured herself a lot of whisky. She sat in a chair opposite Graham and took a large swig. He seemed quiet and almost sober. Maybe he was acting a bit when he came through the window—making it slightly better for her by pretending to be more drunk than he was. A strange considerateness, if so.

How odd life's causes and effects were, she thought. Jack pats my bum and Graham throws a garden fork through the french window. What sort of logical response to anything was that? Or the bigger connection: years ago I had a normally nice time enjoying myself, and because of it my normally nice husband, whom I didn't even know then, is going crackers.

She tried to remember that Graham was essentially nice. All her friends agreed, especially her women friends. He was gentle; he was clever; he didn't strut and preen and bully in the way that many of his sex did. That's what her friends had said, and Ann would delightedly have agreed with them. Until now. Gradually, Graham had stopped seeming as different from other men as he once had. She didn't feel he was interested in her any more. He'd turned into a man like other men: lovingly surprised at his own emotions, while diminishing those of his partner. He'd reverted.

And how remorselessly he'd managed to move himself to the centre of the stage. She knew about the tyranny of the weak: that had been one of her first discoveries about relationships. She'd also discovered, slowly, about the tyranny of the nice: how the virtuous screw their allegiance out of the vicious. Now Graham was teaching her a new one: the tyranny of the passive. That was what he was exercising; and she'd bloody had enough.

'Graham,' she said, addressing him for the first time since he'd come through the window, 'have you ever been to a brothel?'

He looked across at her. What could she mean? Of course he hadn't been to a brothel. Even the word had a fusty smell to it. He hadn't heard it for years. It took him back to his student days, when he and his friends—virgins every one of them—used to bid each other public goodnight with a cheery 'See you down the brothel'. To which you shouted back, 'Maisie's or Daisy's?'

'Of course I haven't.'

'Well, do you know what they used to do in brothels? I read it somewhere.' Ann took another swig of her drink; she felt a flicker of something approaching sadism as she prolonged the introduction. Graham didn't reply; he shifted his glasses sideways and waited.

'Well, in brothels, what they used to do—I only asked you in case they still did it and you might know—was, sometimes, with the younger girls, they used to make a little bag of blood. Chicken's blood, I think it was, usually, though I shouldn't think it mattered. More important, the bag had to be made out of some very thin material. Nowadays, maybe they use polythene. No, I don't suppose they would. I mean, polythene's actually quite tough, isn't it?'

Graham carried on waiting. His head felt quite clear now, though his arm ached.

'And the girl would pop it up herself, and the other women would get going, I think with ordinary candle wax, and they'd seal her up. And then they'd sell her as a virgin. If she looked too old they'd say she'd been in a nunnery and had just come out—sometimes they'd dress her as a nun for an extra turn-on. And the client would push his way past the candle wax—I dare say they used beeswax in the better class of brothel—and the girl would give a yelp and flinch and squeeze her thighs together and burst the bag and sob a little and mutter some crap to make the man feel powerful and conquering but most of all *first*. And then he would leave an extra big tip because he'd left his indelible mark, this was what he'd been saving up for and he'd had it and the girl hadn't actually gone psychotic on him.'

Graham felt, whatever was coming, that he'd somehow deserved it.

'Of course, it was more expensive, because the chicken's blood would mess up the sheets, but then they were paying more anyway, for the virgin, and I guess the brothels had some cut-price deal with the laundries. They must have got through an awful lot of sheets, mustn't they?'

Graham's continuing silence, intended to convey understanding of Ann's need for aggression, struck her as wet. That word kept easing itself into her mind. Fucking *wet*, she thought, fucking *wet*.

'I wonder if laundries actually *know* they're dealing with brothels. I mean, do you think they use extra bleach on the sheets? Do they say, here come the brothel sheets — get out the biological. Do you think they say that, Graham? I'm not asking you to do more than speculate. Is that what you think they do? Or do you think they simply treat brothel sheets like everyone else's? Just bulk washing and never mind what gets left on them?'

Ann got up and walked across to Graham's chair. He kept his head down. Finally he spoke.

'Yes?'

'Yes to what? I've asked you a lot of questions. Which one have you kindly agreed to answer? Yes to Have you ever been to a brothel: was it that Yes?'

'No. I just meant, what is it?'

'What is it? Ah, what is it? Well, I'm glad you've noticed it's something. Well, what it *is*, Graham, what it *is*, is I was just thinking maybe we should buy a chicken for dinner soon. Not one of those all-washed-out ones that have been hosed through and scraped off and injected with stuff to make them taste chickeny. But a real chicken, you know, a HEN, a HEN with feathers and feet and that red thing on the top of its head. And then you could chop it up and we could drain off some of the blood. And then we could melt some candlewax together, and one night, one special night, I could be your virgin, Graham. You'd like that, wouldn't you?'

He didn't reply. He kept looking down. Ann stared at the top of his head.

'I could be your virgin,' she repeated.

Graham was immobile. She reached down and touched his hair; he flinched, and moved his head away. Then she repeated once more, and more softly this time,

'I could be your virgin.'

Graham got up slowly, and deftly threaded his way past his wife, swaying to avoid her body, and especially her eyes, then again to avoid the coffee table. He kept looking at the carpet until he was safely at the door; then quickened his pace as he walked upstairs. He locked his study door and sat down in his chair. He didn't come to bed all night. He sat in his chair, thinking of all that had happened since the honey time began. Why couldn't you unknow knowledge? Call back yesterday, he wailed quietly to himself. At about four o'clock he fell asleep. There were no dreams to be had that short night.

# TEN

# *The Stanley Spencer Syndrome*

Some years ago Graham had read a fashionable work of popular zoology. Everyone cited it at the time, and some had even dipped into it. The book proved in the first part that man was very similar to lots of animals, and in the second part that he was very different. It gave you first an atavistic frisson, and then a pat on the back; it sold in millions. One detail came back to Graham: the fact that man owns not just the biggest brain of all the primates, but also the biggest penis. This had struck him as bafflingly wrong at the time — the time being when he was still tormented daily by Barbara with her net and trident, when he kept moving crabwise away from her but always tripped in the sand. Now, it seemed to make sense. It was no longer paradoxical that a huge gorilla had a tiny cock, outgunned by even the most minuscule of Graham's students. Size didn't relate to prowess or need: it related to the trouble factor. It hung there between your legs as a warning: Don't expect me not to bite back.

On the one hand, of course, sex didn't matter at all, especially not sex in the past, sex in history. On the other hand, it mattered completely; it mattered more than everything else put together. And Graham didn't see how this state of affairs was ever going to change. It had all been decided for him up there in his brain, without consultation, years ago; decided by sodding history and his background and his parents' choice of one another — by the unprecedented combination of genes they had thrust at him and told him to get on with.

Jack, needless to say, had got a better deal. Graham used to think that his friend was more relaxed about things simply because of his wider experience, his earned cynicism. Now he didn't believe so: the rules were all set much earlier. Jack's Parking Fine Principle, for instance, was the sort of precept Graham could never arrive at himself however long he lived, however frantic his activity. Jack had once been expounding his 'maximum stealth, maximum kindness' theory when Graham had broken in,

'But you do get caught?'

'No—much too careful. None of this into-the-closet-with-you stuff for me. That's strictly for kids. At my age it'd strain the ticker too much.'

'I meant, Sue does find out sometimes, doesn't she?'

'Sort of. A bit. When I forget to tuck the tail of my shirt in.'

'And what do you do then? What do you say to her?'

'Use the Parking Fine Principle.'

' ... ?'

'Remember when parking meters came in? And it was all the latest technology—fines handled by computers: remember? Chum of mine discovered, quite by chance, that you could pile up lots of tickets, pay the most recent one, and the computer would automatically wipe out its memory of the earlier ones. That's the Parking Fine Principle. Tell them about the latest, and they stop worrying their littles about the earlier ones.'

And he'd said it not cynically, or disparagingly, but with what sounded like a crisp fondness for the objects of his deceptions. That was how it was; that was how he was; that was how Graham could never be.

The clinching evidence Graham had been looking for was suggested in a simple, obvious way. He was sitting in the

Odeon Holloway Road watching, for the third time that week, his wife committing onscreen adultery with Tony Rogozzi in *The Fool Who Found Fortune*. Rogozzi played an ordinary Italian barrow-boy given at weekends to combing the agricultural land of the Home Counties with a metal detector. One day he discovers a hoard of old coins and his life changes. He forsakes his barrow and his religion, buys lurex suits, tries to lose his comic Italian accent, and becomes estranged from his family and his fiancée. While spending his money in nightclubs he discovers Graham's wife, with whom he has an affair, despite parental warnings:

'She only wanna sucka you dry, bambino,' counsels his father between forkfuls of spaghetti, 'an thenna she tossa you away like an old shoe.'

Tony, however, perseveres in his infatuation, giving Ann expensive presents which she feigns to admire but immediately sells. But just as he is about to cash all his coins and leave his roots for ever, his parents receive two visitors: a policeman to explain that all the coins are stolen property anyway; and Ann's old mother, who selflessly declares that her daughter is a callous gold-digger who has been openly boasting of skinning a naive young Italian. Tony, sadder but wiser, returns to his family, his fiancée, and his barrow. During the final scene, in which Tony and his fiancée together vandalize the metal detector (rather like Adam and Eve chopping up the serpent, Graham thought), the largely Italian audience in the Odeon Holloway Road clapped and cheered.

While the rest of them absorbed a moral lesson, Graham picked up a practical idea. At one point, as Rogozzi crouched nearer the recently bejewelled Ann in a deep-buttoned restaurant, enviously watching the candlelight probe her cleavage, the temporarily lapsed barrow-boy whispered,

'Angelica,' (it was not her real name, but one assumed for the purposes of gulling him) 'Angelica, I writa you a poem, likea my fellow-countryman Dante. He havea his Beatrice' (he pronounced the name as if it were his favourite pasta) 'an Iya havea my Angelica.'

Gotcha, Graham thought as he came out. Now if the affair began in what, 1970, 1971, that would mean there were five possible sources in which to look. Jack couldn't have kept quiet in all of them. For a start, he simply wasn't an inventive enough writer: if he wanted a bus conductor for a short scene, he couldn't produce one without taking a bus ride. The conductor would then appear in his pages with some tiny adjustment — a gammy leg, a ginger moustache — which would make Jack feel like Coleridge.

And secondly, Jack's sentimental nature had turned him, as a writer, into a diligent payer of tributes and dues. This streak, at its most basic and self-serving, emerged when Jack had once stood in for six months as a theatre critic.

'Say you have to go to some sodding fringe play in Hammersmith or Peckham or wherever,' the novelist had explained. 'You can't get out of it because your editor is keen on all that democratic shitse and you have to pretend to go along with it. You pack the old hip flask and steel yourself for a lot of anguished balls designed to change the face of society in a run of three weeks. You slump in your democratically uncomfortable chair, and after three minutes maximum the old brain is yelling, "Let me out of here." You're not enjoying yourself; sure, you're getting paid to be there, but that's not enough. It's just not enough. So you pick out the best bit of crumpet in the play and decide she's "a new discovery". You start with one of those whingy intros praising yourself for having gone to the Tramshed Theatre Dalston, and then you piss on the play a bit, and then you say, "But the evening was redeemed for me by a stunning moment of pure theatre, a moment of perfect beauty and touching emotion, when Daphne O'Twat, playing the third mill-weaver, strokes her machine as if it were a beloved pet — which, in those bleak times, it probably was; the gesture, and the strange, faraway look in her eye, transcend the grime and back-breaking labour of those suffering forbears of ours, and cut through to the most cynical in the audience in a moment which arches over the brooding sky of this play like a bursting rainbow."

'Notice that I don't say Miss O'Twat has got terrific tits or a face like the Venus de Milo. Your editor might rumble it, not to mention the girl concerned. Doing it this way, the editor just says, "Hey, let's get a mug of this chick" and sends off a photog, while the girl thinks, "This could be my big break — a rave notice which *doesn't* mention my tits." So the day after the piece comes out you ring up the Ditchwater in the Round, get on to Dilys O'Muff, say you're coming down because you've just got to see her deeply spiritual performance all over again, and what about having a deeply spiritual jar with you afterwards. Then you're away. Doesn't always work. Works often enough, though.'

This was Jack's 'tribute' system at its crudest. But he also liked to decorate his more serious texts with what he called 'toasts and teases'. The toasts were hidden moments of praise for his friends and heroes; the teases were points at which he rubbished people he disliked. It made writing more fun, Jack insisted. 'Gives you an extra motivation when you feel you've hewn enough truth for one day.'

Graham knelt in front of Ann's shelves. There were ten of them: The Works of Jack Lupton. Five he didn't need; the other five, starting with *Out of the Dark*, he removed. To cover up the hole in the shelves, he pushed up Doris Lessing on one side and Alison Lurie on the other; then fetched a couple of his own Mary McCarthys and shoved them in further along. That looked okay.

He carried the five novels up to his study. He hadn't skimmed books in the way he was doing now since adolescence. In those days, too, he'd been skimming for sex: after all, fiction was where you went when parents and encyclopaedias failed. A practised eye could make words like 'brassière', 'bosom' and 'loins' stand out from the text as if printed in bold type. This time, there were no obvious key words to look for.

Thank God he didn't have to wade through Jack's first five books. The first three — 'my Lincolnshire poacher days' as Jack would mock-modestly categorize them — were taken up with what the novelist called 'the task of putting my family on the fictive shelf'. Next came three 'novels of sexual and political conflict', the last of which Graham would have to flip through. Finally there were the latest four, where the social, political and sexual ambitions and guilts which animated the first six had died away, where all the characters took on a cynical wash, where it didn't really matter who did what to whom, and whether things ended well or ill: they were moving towards stylized comedies of manners in high-bohemian settings. Soon, Graham hoped, Jack would turn into a latter-day Firbank, which would not only amount to a neat revenge on the reputedly earthy writer, but also ensure that nobody would ever want to read or publish Lupton ever again. And by that time he would be so pickled in his own manner that he'd be unable to change.

The last of the politico-sexual novels, *Out of the Dark*, had been published in 1971. In it, Graham remembered, Jack was lightly disguised as a bearded junior minister who, shortly before election time, engages in a liaison with Sarah, an attractive lobby correspondent; his ten-year marriage to a competent home-maker has begun to stale. Soon, the wife finds out and starts blackmailing the Jack-figure: either give up the girl, or I'll expose you to the papers and make sure you lose both your marginal seat and custody of the children. 'Jack' prepares to defy convention and put his case before the electorate and the divorce courts, when Sarah selflessly argues the case for the Party (even though, ironically, it is not *her* party) and the children (another irony, since she is pregnant by 'Jack' but hasn't told him, and intends having a secret abortion). 'Jack' is finally persuaded that there are times when principles must hold sway over the call of the heart; when Sarah heroically leaks to him the social security cuts her party plans for after the election, he reflects on the plight of working families and their need for his presence in the next parliament, and finally accepts the correctness of her decision. Before they part, however, they make love one last time:

> Jock [as Jack was called in the novel] caught her with urgent force. He was as capable of being fierce and demanding as he was of being soft and gentle. This time he was fierce and demanding. Sarah knew him in both modes, loved him in both modes. As he pushed himself on top of her, she breathed deep the rough male smell of cigarette smoke emanating from his beard. This excited her. She had had enough in her time of namby-pamby after-shave exquisites—men who looked like men but might as well be women.
> 'Jock,' she murmured in protest as his hand roughly pushed at her skirt.
> 'Yes, yes,' he replied urgently, commandingly. 'Here. Now.'
> And there, then, on the sofa, roughly he took her. He would brook no protest, and found indeed that his imperious desire had provoked in Sarah an answering wetness. He kissed the small mole on the left side of her neck, and she raised her loins to him. Then, fiercely, and still wearing the brown tweed suit which had been made from cloth woven in his constituency, he entered her gathered her up in his strength, and launched them both, higher than ever before—high, high above the earth, through the clouds to where you find the sun and where the sky is always blue. At the peak of their transport he gave a great cry, as of a wounded beast, and a small tear escaped the confines of her right eye.
> 'Jock,' she whispered, 'there'll never be another ... '
> 'No,' he replied with gentle mastery, 'there will ... '

'Never,' she cried, almost in pain.

'Not now,' he assured her, 'not soon. But sometime, there will be another. And I shall want it that way too. I shall still be out there, somewhere, wanting it for you.'

He quieted her last protests and, still inside her, reached into his jacket and handed her a cigarette. Absently, she placed the untipped end in her mouth and waited for him to light the cork. Gently, he took it from her lips, and turned it round. She was always doing that … As he lit the proper end, he noticed a slight smear of lipstick on it — the final, melancholy smear, he reflected, that had escaped being rubbed off in their soaring exchange of kisses …

Pages 367 and 368: Graham ripped them out. The clues were unmissable: the tear in the eye — that had happened a few times; the lifting of the bottom — yes; the clincher, though, was the mole — even if he had moved it from her right shoulder to the left side of her neck (this would be what Jack called imagination). And even if the mole wasn't a clincher, there was the cigarette. Ann often put cigarettes into her mouth the wrong way round. Graham hadn't ever noticed her doing it after they made love, but she'd done it several times when socially flustered. Hadn't Jack been there on one such occasion? And hadn't there been some shared joke he didn't understand? He couldn't quite remember.

He flipped through *Out of the Dark* for a hundred pages or so on either side of the passage he'd just discovered, and tore out all the other references to Ann's affair with Jack. He could read them through later. Then he turned his attention to the last four Lupton novels. Novellas, really: the start of the neo-Firbank period, Graham repeated gleefully to himself. Jack's explanation was different.

'Used to belong to the Tesco school of fiction,' he had once explained. 'You know: pile it high, sell it cheap. Thought that if people had a choice between some 200-page bit of smart wankery at four quid, or 400 pages of my gutsy stuff at five quid, they'd see which was the better bargain. And I was right of course; they did prefer my stuff. But after half a dozen bleedings of my life's blood, I thought, hey, aren't I screwing myself a bit? It's twice as long, but do I get twice the royalties? Then I saw all these chick novelists turning out monographs, and I thought, Jack boy, you can do that and leave a hand free for what-you-will at the same time. So I did, and you know, I'm beginning to see the point of all this minimalism. It's easy on the bum, that's what.'

In the neo-Firbank period, Jack's toasts and teases continued. A phrase of Ann's; a description of her breasts; a mannerism while making love; a dress. The more evidence Graham found, the easier it became to find yet more; and in the exhilaration of his critical pursuit he seemed to forget the precise significance of what he was finding out.

Only later, when he assembled the torn-out evidence—which added up to half the length of a late-period Lupton—did he stop for thought. Then, as he read through the collected evidence of the Jack–Ann affair, as he watched Ann's body arch up towards Jack, and Jack stick his smelly beard into Ann's face in the mistaken belief that stale nicotine was an aphrodisiac (it *couldn't* be, Graham insisted, it couldn't be), the anaesthetic wore off and the pains returned. He held his stomach with one hand, his chest with the other, and rocked forwards as he sat on the floor by the torn-out pages. Then he began slipping sideways and he keeled over into a foetal position; his hands slipped between his thighs, and he lay on the floor like a sick child. He shut his eyes and tried, as he used to when he was a boy, to think of something different, external, exciting. He thought of a game of village cricket, until the spectators turned into a football crowd chanting 'Carwash, carwash'. He thought of abroad, until Benny drove by in his silver Porsche on the way to Arezzo, and casually flung a pair of knickers out of the window. He thought of giving a class on Bonar Law, until all his students put their hands up at the same time and demanded to go into the film industry. Finally, he thought of his childhood, back before Ann and Jack and Barbara, back to the time when there had only been his parents to pacify; the years before betrayal existed, when there was only tyranny and subservience. He worked hard at holding in place the memory of that circumscribed time; gradually he retreated into it and pulled its certainties up around his ears; and then he fell asleep.

Over the next few days Graham read and re-read the passages from *Out of the Dark* and the later works. There could be no doubt at all. Jack's affair with Ann had started in 1971, had continued during the time he was first getting to know Ann, and then through all their marriage. *Hot Certainties*, *The Doused Fire* and *Rage, Rage* contained the necessary evidence. If he allowed six months — a year at maximum — for the publishers to produce the book, this meant that the passages in *The Doused Fire* where 'Jack', lightly disguised as an ex-bomber pilot whose face has been refashioned by plastic surgery, has a healing relationship with 'Ann', a Scottish nurse with a mole in the right place for once, were written during the first year of their marriage. The infidelity didn't even lapse then, Graham thought; not even then.

A week or so later, Graham telephoned Sue in the country, having first prepared himself to wrong-number Jack if by any chance he answered.

'Sue, it's Graham.'

'Graham ... oh, Graham.' She sounded relieved at having guessed the right Graham, rather than actually pleased. 'Jack's in London.'

'Yes, I know. I wanted to talk to you.'

'Go ahead. I'm not all that busy.' She still didn't sound welcoming.

'Could we meet, Sue? In London one day?'

'Graham ... well ... what's it about?'

'I don't want to tell you now.'

'Just as long as it isn't something you think I ought to know. As long as you don't think you know what's good for me.'

'It's not like that. It's sort of, well, about you and me ... ' He did sound serious.

'Graham, I didn't know you cared. Better late than never, anyway.' She gave a skittish giggle. 'Let me look at my diary. Yes, just as I thought. I can offer you any day between now and the end of the decade.'

They fixed on a date a week ahead.

'Oh and Sue ... '

'Yes?'

'Would you think it odd if I said ... if I said I hope you don't tell Jack we're having lunch together.'

'He has his own life,' she replied sharply. 'I have mine.'

'Of course.'

Could her implication have been clearer, Graham wondered as he put down the phone. Yes, he supposed it could, but even so ... Especially as he'd rung her completely out of the blue. He hadn't seen her for over a year and, well, after all, he didn't really like her much, did he? That natural vivacity which friends praised was a bit close, in Graham's view, to unfocused aggression.

The following week he sat in Tardelli's over a Campari and soda, at a table tucked away round a corner. He pondered the best way to get the final corroboration he sought. He couldn't just ask for it, that was certain.

'Graham, darling, the adulterers' table — you *were* serious.'

' ... ?'

'You mean you didn't know?' She was still holding her face out towards him. He half-rose, kicking a table leg as he did so, and touched his lips to her cheek. Had they been on kissing terms before? He wasn't sure.

'I asked for a quiet table,' he replied, 'I said we wanted an undisturbed lunch.'

'So you didn't know that this is the official adulterers' table?'

'No, really.'

'How disappointing.'

'But no one can see you here.'

'That's just the point. You're out of sight, but in order to get to the table or go for a pee or anything, you have to declare yourself to the whole restaurant. It's famous, darling —maybe not in your circles, but certainly in ours.'

'You mean people deliberately sit here?'

'Of course. It's much pleasanter than putting an announcement in *The Times*. It's a brilliant form of discreet publicity, I always think. You announce a liaison while pretending to yourself to be hiding it. Eases the guilt, but gets the news around. Ideal solution. I'm surprised more restaurants don't have tables like this.'

'Is there likely to be anyone here you know?' Graham wasn't sure whether to act pleased or apprehensive.

'Who can tell? Don't worry, love, I'll take care of you when they pop their heads round the corner and pretend to be looking for someone else.' She patted his arm reassuringly.

After that, Graham decided there was only one way to let the lunch run. He acted the shy flirt, risking an occasional light touch, and gauchely getting caught stealing glances at her. Distantly, genially, he went along with the received opinion that she was a pretty woman; but he didn't confront the question very seriously.

Since Graham had not, it seemed, come to discuss her husband's infidelities, that was precisely what Sue talked to him about. Since he had not come to press his cause with a today-or-forget-it urgency, she talked, as an analogue, about her own occasional affairs; about the difficulties of conducting any liaison in the country without being found out; and about her townee's fears of bucolic revenge, of pitchforks, and balers, and feed silos. For a moment, as the second carafe was emptied and they were waiting for their coffee, Sue's tone hardened.

'You know what I call the way Jack goes on? I call it the Stanley Spencer syndrome. Know about that?'

Graham indicated that he didn't.

'And the fact that I was Jack's second wife makes it even more appropriate.' She lit a cigarette. 'When Stanley Spencer got married for the second time, do you know what happened on the wedding night?'

'No.'

'He sent his new wife ahead on the honeymoon, like an advance crate of luggage, went home, and fucked his first wife.'

'But ... '

'No, no, wait for it. Not that. Then he went off to join his second wife and sat her down on the beach and explained to her that an artist had exceptional sexual needs, and that he now proposed to keep two wives. His art required it, and his art came first. Cold-blooded little dwarf,' she added, as if Spencer were a drinking companion of her husband's. 'And that's what Jack's got, to a certain extent. He's smart enough not to put it like that, but deep down it's what he believes. Sometimes when I'm at home I stand in front of the row of books he's written and I find myself thinking, I wonder how many fucks went into that one?'

'Well, you know what Balzac used to say —"There goes another novel." ' Graham felt uneasy, not sure whether this remark was reassuring or the opposite.

'And then I have another look at the books, and I think about Jack screwing around all these years, and I think, I don't really mind *that* much, not after the first hurt of it, and after all I've had some fun myself, but what I really resent when I look at his ten novels lined up on the shelf, what I really can't forgive him for, is that they aren't bloody better than they are. I sometimes feel like saying to him, "Look, Jack, you can forget the books, just forget them. They aren't that good. Give them up and concentrate on the screwing. You're better at that." '

Graham thought of the torn-out sections of *Rage, Rage*, *The Doused Fire* and *Out of the Dark*. Then he began what he had very carefully prepared.

'Sue, I hope you won't misunderstand me. I thought it would be nice to ... to ... ' he stumbled a bit, deliberately, 'to have lunch with you, to see you, because we've been out of touch for a while, and I've always thought we, I, don't see enough of you. I don't want you to think I've got some motive of neatness, or revenge or anything.' She looked puzzled, and he hurried on. 'I mean, we all knew about Jack and Ann in the old days, and that's not at all surprising, and anyway, if they hadn't been, um, lovers then I might not have met her, so I suppose in a way I'm even sort of a bit grateful.' Graham felt his show of timid honesty was going quite well; now came the tricky part.

'But I *did* get a shock, I have to admit it, when I found out they'd never really stopped having an affair. It gave me quite a stab. I only discovered about six months ago. Apart from anything to do with Ann, I felt a sense of friendship betrayed, and all those emotions people tell us are old-fashioned. I was quite bitter about Jack for a while, but I suppose in a way it's helped me understand Ann's ... needs a bit more. I suppose if I'd rung you then you'd have had reason to doubt my purpose. But, well, that hiccup is over, and I'm quite resigned to it, and then when I found myself thinking how nice it would be to see you again, I examined my motives and once I could give them a clean bill of health I got on the phone. And ... and here we are now, I suppose you could say.'

Graham looked down at his empty coffee cup. He was pleased with the cautious, limp ending. Pushing two separate lines at the same time was a good idea. Just when he was wondering if he dared look up, Sue leaned across and placed a hand on his forearm. He raised his head and met a bright smile.

'I suppose you could.' She liked his shyness. She smiled,

encouragingly, once more, and all the time she was thinking, The bastard, the bastard, the fucking Stanley Spencer Jack Lupton bastard. Why hadn't she guessed? Jack never really gave up his old girlfriends. Maybe he thought they'd stop buying his books if he stopped fucking them. But she clamped down on these feelings. Mustn't let Graham see that she was upset, that she hadn't known, that it would need a hell of a lot more than a few fake smiles on a Friday night to pacify her this time. Don't spoil your chances, girl, don't splash the water; this one will have to be reeled in gently.

'Maybe I should have told you,' she went on, 'but I'm afraid I always work on the cancer rule. If they don't ask, you don't tell them; and if they do ask but really want to be told No, then you still say No. I'm sorry you had to find out from a third party, Graham.'

He smiled wanly, thinking of his deception. She smiled sympathetically, thinking of hers. Sue thought that revenge-fucking Graham might prove quite salutary.

'I hope you won't think me old-fashioned,' he said, continuing his act, 'but I've actually got to take a class in about an hour. Can we, can we meet again next week perhaps?'

Sue found his lack of presumption charming. None of those terrible lines chaps sometimes used, like 'Keep the afternoon free' and 'I'm a bachelor at the moment'. She leaned across and kissed him on the lips. He looked surprised.

'*That*'s the advantage of the adulterers' table,' she said cheerfully. She was pleased he hadn't tried to grope her or anything during lunch. She hoped this passiveness didn't go too far. Still, it made a nice change. Jack, for instance, by this stage would be under the table, his beard bringing a rash like razor-burn to some gullible tart's inner thighs. Would Graham take his glasses off in bed?

They kissed goodbye outside the restaurant, Sue already with her mind on the same time, same place, the next week, and whatever might follow. Graham was also looking ahead, but in quite a different direction.

# ELEVEN

# *The Horse and the Crocodile*

It was only offal, Graham found himself repeating under his breath as he drove to Repton Gardens. It was all offal. Well, not quite all, but it was the offal that came out on top. He'd spent forty years fighting it, and could now perceive the irony of his life: that the years when he'd thought of himself as a failure — when the whole mechanism seemed to be quietly and painlessly running down — were in fact the time of success.

It was clever stuff, offal, he reflected as he passed the Staunton Road carwash for the hundredth time since it all began. Clever stuff. And of course he hadn't been a pushover: that's why he had lasted forty years in the first place. It got to other people much more quickly. But it got to everyone in the end. With him it had taken the long, slow, circuitous route, and finally chosen someone quite unexpected as its instrument. Ann, who loved him; whom he loved.

It hadn't changed much since the Middle Ages, since Montaillou, since the time they believed literally in offal: in blood, liver, bile, and so on. What was the latest theory which Jack — Jack of all people — had explained to him? That there were two or three different layers of the brain constantly at war with one another. This was only a different way of saying that your guts fucked you up, wasn't it? All it meant was that the battle-plan and the metaphor had shifted about two feet six up your body.

And the battle was always lost, that was what Graham had been taught to recognize. The offal came out on top. You could delay it for a while, by desiccating your life as much as possible; though this only made you more of a prize later. The real division in the world wasn't between those who had lost the battle and those who hadn't yet fought it; but between those who, when they lost the battle, could accept defeat, and those who couldn't. Maybe there was some little broom-cupboard of the brain where *that* was decided too, he reflected with glum irritation. But people did divide that way. Jack, for instance, accepted his defeat, didn't seem to notice really, even turned it to his advantage. Whereas Graham couldn't accept it now, and knew he would never be able to. Which was also ironic, because Jack was altogether a more pugnacious and truculent character; Graham saw himself as something very close to the mild, amiable, slightly put-upon figure that others perceived.

'Ah, mmm, telephone,' Jack muttered, answering the door after some considerable time. Then he hurried off down the hall.

'No, my little coronary,' Graham could hear as he took off his mac and hung it on the peg. 'No, look, not now, I'll ring you back ... ' Graham patted his jacket pockets ' ... don't know. Not too long ... arriveheari.'

Graham reflected that even a few days ago he might have been interested in whoever Jack was talking to; might it be Ann? Now, it simply didn't matter. There could have been a trail of familiar underclothes smirking at him from the stairs and still Graham wouldn't have been bothered.

Jack seemed a bit flustered. 'Just a little birdie whispering in my ear,' he said jovially by way of explanation. 'Come in, corky.' He grinned uneasily. Turning into the sitting-room, he farted, for once without commentary.

'Coffee?' Graham nodded.

It had only been a few months since he'd been sitting in the same chair, tremulously offering to Jack his fretful ignorances. Now he sat, listening to Jack tinkling at the coffee mugs with a spoon, and felt he knew it all. Not knew it all in the straightforward factual sense — about Jack and Ann, for instance — but knew it all in the wider sense. In the old stories, people grew up, struggled, had misfortunes, and eventually came to ripeness, to a sense of being at ease with the world. Graham, after forty years of not struggling very much, felt he had come to ripeness in a few months, and irrevocably grasped that terminal unease was the natural condition. This sudden wisdom had disconcerted him at first; now he felt calm about it. As he pushed his hand into his jacket pocket, he admitted that he might be misunderstood; he might be thought of as merely jealous, merely crackers. Well, that was up to them.

And the advantage of probably being misunderstood in any case, he said to himself as Jack handed him a mug, was that you didn't have to explain. You really didn't. One of the more contemptible features of the flicks he'd been going to see in recent months was the smug convention under which characters were called upon to explain their motives. 'I killed you because I loved you too much,' blubbed the lumberjack with the dripping chainsaw. 'I felt this great like ocean of hate man welling up inside of me, and I had to ex-*plode*,' puzzled the violent but likable black teenage arsonist. 'I guess I never could get Daddy out of my system, that's why I fell for you,' frankly admitted the now dissatisfied bride. Graham had winced at such moments, at the haughty gap between life and dramatic convention. In life you didn't have to explain if you didn't want to. Not because there was no audience: there was, and one habitually thirsty for motive at that. It was just that they didn't have any rights; they hadn't paid any box-office money to your life.

So I don't have to say anything. What's more, it's important that I don't. Jack might drag me off into camaraderie, and then where would I be? Probably nowhere different, but compromised, halfway towards being explained, towards being sodding understood.

'Anything up, matey?'

Jack was gazing across at him with benign irritation. Since he seemed to be running this counselling service now, he wished the buggers would stick to a few normal rules. Didn't they realize he had a job? Did they think all those books of his just turned up one morning at the foot of the chimney, and that all he had to do was dust the soot off them and send them round to the publishers? Is that what they thought? And now, they not only turned up without any warning, they just sat there like blocks of stone. Othello was turning into what's his name—Ozymandias.

'Cough, cough,' said Jack. Then, with a more hesitating jokiness, he repeated into Graham's silence, 'Cough, cough?'

Graham looked across and smiled distantly. He gripped his mug more fiercely than he needed to, and took a sip.

'Coffee to your satisfaction, *sah*?' enquired Jack.

Still nothing.

'I mean, I don't mind earning my thirty guineas this way; it's no skin off my fore. I should imagine every shrink would envy me you. It's just that it's a bit boring. I mean, if I *am* to put you in my next novel, I've got to feel more what's going on inside you, haven't I?'

*Put you in my next novel* ... Oh yes, and will you give me a mole on the end of my nose so that I won't recognize myself? Make me thirty-nine instead of forty-two? Some sophisticated little touch like that? But Graham resisted the temptation to ironic reply. Instead, he worried about his hands getting damp.

Suddenly, Jack picked up his coffee and walked to the other end of his long room. He sat down on his piano stool, shifted some of the garbage round, lit a cigarette and switched on his typewriter. Graham listened to the low electric hum, then the rapid clatter of the keys. It didn't sound like a proper typewriter to him, more like one of those things which announced sports results on television—what was it, a teleprinter? Well, that wasn't inappropriate: nowadays Jack's fiction was produced more or less automatically. Maybe there was a special switch on his machine, like the autopilot on an aeroplane: Jack only had to press it and his teleprinter would churn out autojunk.

'Don't mind me,' Jack called out over the hum. 'Stay as long as you like.'

Graham looked down the sitting-room. The novelist was sitting with his back to him; Graham could just see the right side of his face and a bit of fuzzy brown beard. He could almost make out the spot where Jack lodged his cigarettes in that reckless but oh-so-charming way of his. 'Anyone smell burning?' he'd say with such a straight face, and the object of that particular night's pursuit would whinny with delight at this strange, absent-minded, self-destructive but obviously creative person. Graham wished he'd been able to tell some of them about the autojunk switch on the typewriter.

'Get yourself some more coffee whenever you like,' Jack called out. 'Lots of stuff in the deep freeze if you're counting on staying a few days. Spare bed's made up.'

Well it would be. You never knew when it would come in useful. Not that Jack would have any scruples about dousing the marital bed.

In a funny way Graham was just as fond of Jack as he'd always been. But that had absolutely nothing to do with the case. He set his coffee down on the floor and quietly stood up. Then he walked slowly across towards the desk. The hum and the occasional burst of key-clatter covered his steps. He wondered what sort of sentence Jack was in the process of tapping out; he hoped, in a sentimental way, that he wasn't striking in mid-cliché.

It was his favourite: the one with the black bone handle, and a six-inch blade tapering from a breadth of an inch to a sharp point. As he withdrew it from his pocket, he turned it sideways, so that it would slide in between the ribs more easily. He walked the last few feet and then, instead of stabbing, seemed merely to walk into Jack with the knife held out ahead of him. He aimed about halfway up the back on the right-hand side. The knife struck something hard, then slipped downwards a little, then went in suddenly to about half its length.

Jack gave a curious falsetto wheeze, and one of his hands fell on the keyboard. There was a spurt of typing, then a dozen keys got tangled up and the noise stopped. Graham looked down and saw that the jarring entry of the blade had cut the top of his index finger. He pulled out the knife, quickly lifting his eyes away as it emerged.

Jack twisted on the stool, his left elbow dragging on the typewriter and sending a few more keys to join the clogged bunch which were still straining to reach the paper. As the bearded face came slowly round, Graham finally lost control. He stabbed repeatedly at Jack's lower body, at the area which lay between the heart and the genitals. After several blows, Jack rolled soundlessly off the piano stool on to the carpet; but this didn't placate Graham. Shifting his grip so that he could stab downwards, he worked doggedly away at the same area. Between the heart and the genitals, that was what he wanted. Between the heart and the genitals.

Graham didn't have any idea how many times he stabbed Jack. He just stopped when the knife seemed to be going in more easily, when resistance, not from Jack, but from his body, appeared to have stopped. He took the knife out for the last time and wiped it on Jack's sweater. Then he placed it flat on his friend's chest, went to the kitchen and rinsed his hand. He found some Elastoplast and stretched it awkwardly over the top joint of his finger. After that he went back to his chair, sat down, leaned over the arm and picked up his coffee. There was half a mug left, and it was still warm. He settled down to drink it.

At seven o'clock Ann arrived home, expecting cooking smells, a large drink in Graham's wavering hand, and another evening of tears and recriminations. She had stopped thinking about things getting better, or how to make them do so. Instead, she took each day by itself and tried to hold on to the right memories as the evenings degenerated. She took faith from a couple of things. The first was a belief that no one could go on being fuelled by such negative emotions for ever. The second was the realization that only rarely did Graham seem to be directly reproaching her: *her now*, that is. He was hostile to a past her, to a present situation, but not to a present her. These sources of comfort, she found, worked best when Graham wasn't there. When he was there, it seemed much more likely that the situation might continue for ever, and that Graham genuinely hated her.

At eight o'clock Ann rang Graham's head of department, to be told that, as far as he knew, Graham had worked his normal day and gone home in the mid-afternoon. Would she like the home number of the department's secretary? Ann didn't think that was necessary.

At eight-ten she rang Jack, and got no reply.

She hoped Graham hadn't started another burst of going to films.

At ten o'clock, against her will, she rang Barbara and got Alice. After two seconds she got Barbara.

'I don't think it's a good idea for you to talk to *my* daughter, thank you very much, she's all I've got now you've taken my husband away from me.' It was doubtless intended to be overheard by Alice.

'I'm sorry, I didn't know she would answer the phone.'

'I don't want you ringing here in any case.'

'No. I quite understand.'

'You understand? Oh well, that must be nice for you. It gives me quite a thrill to know that at least the woman who stole my husband *understands*. Maybe you understand me better than I do myself, maybe you stole Graham from me for my own good.'

Ann always felt sympathy for Barbara until she needed to have any dealing with her, however indirect. Then she felt exhausted almost straight away. Why did Barbara enjoy complication so much?

'I just wondered—I just wondered if you'd heard from Graham.'

'Heard? Why should I? It's not Thursday.'

'No, I mean, he hasn't come home. I wondered if he'd … he'd been round to take Alice out or something.'

There was a laugh, then a stagy sigh from the other end of the phone.

'Well, well, well. *Since* you ask, No I haven't seen Graham, No I would never let him see Alice except when the court said he could, and No I can't think where he might have got to because' (the tone became crisper) 'the only times he never came home to *me* was when he was shilly-shallying about with *you*. Have you checked his suitcase?'

'What do you mean?'

'Well, let me tell you the pattern, just so you'll recognize it, though I must say I don't think it says much for you if he's already playing up after, what is it, three years, four years? Yes it must be four, because Alice was twelve when he left, I remember telling him how he was running off at a crucial time in the child's development, and as she's sixteen you must have stolen him four years ago. You see, that's how I date things nowadays. You might find yourself doing the same at some stage. The point about the suitcase is, he only ever takes one suitcase. Just a few clothes, not even his toothbrush. I suppose he feels less guilty that way. Only the one suitcase, so it's not a bad deal for you in some ways; I got quite a good price for his clobber. Oh, and the other thing is, he makes the taxi wait round the corner. Goes off all long-faced and sighing with his suitcase, and jumps into a cab round the corner. Why not ring the local taxi firm and find out where he's gone to? I mean, that's what *I* did.'

The phone was abruptly put down. Ann felt depressed. Barbara was certainly someone capable of sustaining negative emotions.

At half-past ten she rang Jack again. He was obviously making a night of it.

What were you meant to do? Ring the police? 'Probably met up with an old friend, Ma'm. Drinking man, is he?' She couldn't very well say no to that. But Graham had never been anywhere near this late before.

At a quarter to eleven she went upstairs and pushed open Graham's study door. She hadn't been in here since the night of the party. Automatically she crossed to the window and looked down the garden towards the rockery. In one way, it was a relief that he wasn't there.

Without bothering to close the curtains, she switched on the light. The room wasn't exactly out of bounds to her, but she felt as if she were intruding. This was Graham's private area in their marriage; and not just because he worked here.

She looked around. The desk, the chair, the bookshelves, the filing cabinet. The only thing that had changed was the photograph of her above the desk. Graham used to have a picture of her taken at their wedding — the happiest photo of her ever taken, she thought. Now he had replaced it with one she had almost forgotten giving to him: she was fifteen, awash with puppy fat, an Alice band in her hair, and precariously maintaining on her face a smile which approved of the world and all its doings.

She pushed at one or two of the papers on Graham's desk, not even looking at them. Then she idly pulled open the top drawer of his filing cabinet. 1911–15: full of neatly ordered files. She pulled at the second drawer, 1915–19. It slid out at the lightest of touches, so that she felt barely responsible for having opened it.

A box of Kleenex lay diagonally across a pile of magazines; the top tissue was half pulled out. She pushed the box to one side. The top magazine of a pile of about thirty displayed its back cover: a shiny advert for cigarettes. Ann flipped it over and discovered it was a girlie mag. She delved through the rest of the pile, all of which were face down: different titles, the same widely-stretched contents. So that was why Graham didn't seem keen to fuck her any more.

Or maybe ... or maybe, it was the other way round: he did this precisely because he wasn't keen. Chicken and egg, she thought. As she flicked through the top magazine again, she felt a stirring of unease; her belly contracted. It wasn't that Graham was being unfaithful to her when he came up here, it was just that—just that, yes, in a way he was. It was better, she supposed, than finding a packet of love letters; but she still felt betrayed. Shocked, too: not at what she saw, but at Graham's—at men's—need for it. Why did men have to spell it out so much? Why did they have to bestride their magazines, pseudo-raping dozens of women in one session? Why did they need such coarse visual stimulus? What was wrong with their imagination?

When she pulled out 1919–24 there was a faint smell of almonds, explained by an opened, and now drying, pot of Gripfix. The plastic spatula hadn't been replaced on the spike inside the lid, but lay with a few hard grains of glue on top of a yellow scrapbook. Ann paused, needlessly checking the silence of the house, and then opened it in the middle. She saw two photos of herself—so that's where they went—and some xeroxes of press-cuttings. They were reviews of one of her earliest, and worst, films: reviews which came out years before she met Graham, and none of which mentioned her name. She didn't even have copies of them herself.

She turned on, then back to the beginning and worked her way steadily through the book. It was Graham's secret record of her life before they met: photos; reviews of her films (understandably few of which ever referred to her); xeroxes of a couple of sweater adverts she'd modelled for when she was hard up (how had he found out about *them*?);

even copies of the few occasions—the very few, thankfully —when her name had appeared low down in gossip columns. One of these Graham had circled in red:

> ... also spotted were Jack Lupton, son-of-the-soil author of steamy, between-the-sheets novels, squiring must-try-harder would-be starlet Ann Mears. Mr Lupton's divorce we hear (there are two children) is imminent, but the bearded boyo declined to comment ...

She remembered how sick that had made her feel at the time; how she had suppressed the thought of it on the orders of her agent.

Next to this cutting, which was on a right-hand page, was a drawing in red felt pen of the head of an arrow; the shaft disappeared over the page. She followed it, across a double spread, to where it started: at a review (which had appeared three months before the gossip-page clipping) of *Too Late the Tears*. That crummy film. The review was by Jack. Christ, by Jack. She'd forgotten that entirely. He'd done a brief stint for one of the Sundays as a film critic. And not long afterwards she'd met him at a party. A section of the review was circled in red:

> ... Amid the general smoky nullity of this piece of un-sellable celluloid, there are a few moments which redeem it from causing total bum-numbdom. These are mainly located round Ann Mears, who is well found in an otherwise insignificant part and whose grace arches across this cloudy movie like a bursting rainbow ...

Finally, Ann pulled out 1924–9, with little confidence that she would find there some hidden diary of praise, some sentimental signal of brief happiness. On the left was a cassette from their video-recorder; on the right was a large brown envelope. The cassette was unmarked. She opened the envelope and found bundles of pages which had been torn out of a book; or several books. There were red squiggles down the sides of some of the pages, underlinings and exclamation marks. She half-recognized one of the pages as being from some novel of Jack's, then gradually perceived their communal source. She flipped through them, noticing that almost every page referred to sex in some way.

It was three in the morning by the time she took the cassette downstairs. Cautious prying in Graham's desk had revealed nothing; his bookshelves had disclosed only the five mutilated copies of Jack's novels. Apprehensively she slotted the tape into the V.C.R. and rewound it to the beginning. It started with a commercial for a new brand of chocolate biscuit, in which a kilted servant came up to Queen Victoria and presented her with a packet of the biscuits on a silver tray. She unwrapped them, bit into one, and her plump, mournful face lifted into a smile. 'We are not amazed,' she commented, whereupon a file of kilted courtiers leaped into an eight-second song-and-dance number extolling the biscuit.

Ann had never seen the commercial before. She was to see it again, though. The tape contained eight recordings of the same advert. On the third viewing, she found herself awkwardly aware of something familiar; on the fifth she recognized him, beneath his drooping moustache and drooping tam-o'shanter. Dick Devlin. How had Graham discovered that? Even when she knew that it was Devlin, she could still only just recognize him in the final three recordings. And why the eight versions?

Ann didn't go to bed that night. She replayed the tape, baffled by the secrecy and obsessiveness it implied. Then she went back to the filing cabinet. The only thing she'd missed —because she'd initially taken it for lining paper—was sheet after sheet of the *Evening Standard*. Always the same page: the guide to cinemas. Each one was marked with blurry circlings of red felt pen. Frequently she found that she hadn't even heard of the films marked; any supposed connection they might have with her was incomprehensible.

She leafed once more through the pages torn from Jack's novels, and saw a pattern emerge. But if he thinks all this is about *me*, he's mad, she thought; then checked herself. Graham wasn't mad. Graham was sad; upset; drunk sometimes; but he was not to be called mad. Just as he was not to be called jealous. That was a word she wouldn't use of him. Again, he was sad; upset; he couldn't handle her past; but he wasn't jealous. When Jack had referred to him as 'my little Othello', she'd been annoyed: not just because it was patronizing, but because it disturbed her view of events.

Finally, with some reluctance, she submitted to Barbara's advice and looked in Graham's wardrobe: all his clothes seemed to be there. His suitcase was still there. Of course it would be; of course he hadn't run off.

At ten o'clock the next morning she telephoned the hospitals and the police. Neither had seen him. The police advised her to ring round his friends. They didn't ask if he was a drinking man, though they did say, 'Had a spat by any chance, Ma'm?' She rang work and told them she was feeling queasy. Then, after a final call to Jack's, she walked to the Underground.

The car was outside the flat at Repton Gardens; Graham answered the bell. She instinctively pushed up against him and cast her arms round his waist. He patted her on the shoulder, then turned her into the hallway and kicked the door shut with his left foot. He walked her into the sitting-room; she had to move sideways, awkwardly, but didn't care. When he stopped her she was still looking at his neck, at his profile, his frown. He was gazing past her, towards the other end of the room. She turned, and saw Jack lying beside the piano stool. His sweater had lots of holes in it, and was stained all around the stomach. She saw a knife lying flat on his chest.

Before she could have a proper look Graham, his arm now very firmly round her shoulders, marched her off into the kitchen. As he did so, he muttered the first words he'd spoken since arriving in the flat.

'It's all right.'

The words calmed her, even though she knew they shouldn't. When Graham stood her against the sink, facing out towards the garden, and then pulled her hands behind her back, she didn't object; she let him do it, and waited there while he went away for a few seconds. When he came back he tied her wrists together, not very hard, with one end of a plastic washing line. He left her pointing out towards the garden. Twelve feet of dirty cream washing line trailed from her wrists.

It *was* all right, Graham felt. Apart from it all seeming all wrong, it was all right. He loved Ann, there wasn't any doubt about that, and he hoped she wouldn't turn round. He found his head surprisingly empty of thoughts. The main thing, he said to himself, was for it not to seem like a film: that would be the worst irony of all, and he wasn't having any of that. No curtain lines; no melodrama. He walked across to Jack and picked the knife off his chest. A sudden thought occurred as he straightened up. 'Sometimes a cigar is only a cigar,' he murmured inside his head, 'but sometimes it isn't.' Well, you don't ever really choose, do you, he reflected.

He sat down again in the familiar armchair, and, with a deliberation and courage which surprised him, cut deeply into both sides of his throat. As the blood spurted, he gave an involuntary grunt, which made Ann turn round.

His calculation had been that she would have to run to the phone, kick it over, dial 999 with her hands behind her back, and then wait for someone to arrive. Quite enough time. In fact, Ann immediately ran down the room, trailing the washing line behind her, past the dying Graham, past the dead Jack, round the desk, then put her head down and butted the window as hard as she could. That hurt a lot, but it made a large hole in the window. Then she screamed, as loudly as she could. Not words, but a long, unrelenting, patterned scream. Nobody came, though several people heard. Three of them phoned the police, and one the fire brigade.

Not that it would have made any difference if one of them had got it right. Graham's calculations weren't upset by this variation of event. By the time the first policeman reached inside the broken window to undo the catch, the armchair was irrevocably soaked.

www.vintage-books.co.uk